Traded to the Trucker

BY

Annabelle Winters

Copyright Notice

Copyright © 2020 by Annabelle Winters
All Rights Reserved by Author
www.annabellewinters.com
ab@annabellewinters.com

If you'd like to copy, reproduce, sell, or distribute any part of this text, please obtain the explicit, written permission of the author first. Note that you should feel free to tell your spouse, lovers, friends, and coworkers how happy this book made you. Have a wonderful evening!

Cover Design by S. Lee

ISBN: 9798682936953

0 1 2 3 4 5 6 7 8 9

Books by Annabelle Winters

The CURVES FOR SHEIKHS Series
Curves for the Sheikh
Flames for the Sheikh
Hostage for the Sheikh
Single for the Sheikh
Stockings for the Sheikh
Untouched for the Sheikh
Surrogate for the Sheikh
Stars for the Sheikh
Shelter for the Sheikh
Shared for the Sheikh
Assassin for the Sheikh
Privilege for the Sheikh
Ransomed for the Sheikh
Uncorked for the Sheikh
Haunted for the Sheikh
Grateful for the Sheikh
Mistletoe for the Sheikh
Fake for the Sheikh

The CURVES FOR SHIFTERS Series
Curves for the Dragon
Born for the Bear
Witch for the Wolf
Tamed for the Lion
Taken for the Tiger

The CURVY FOR HIM Series
The Teacher and the Trainer
The Librarian and the Cop
The Lawyer and the Cowboy
The Princess and the Pirate

The CEO and the Soldier
The Astronaut and the Alien
The Botanist and the Biker
The Psychic and the Senator

THE CURVY FOR THE HOLIDAYS SERIES
Taken on Thanksgiving
Captive for Christmas
Night Before New Year's
Vampire's Curvy Valentine
Flagged on the Fourth
Home for Halloween

THE CURVY FOR KEEPS SERIES
Summoned by the CEO
Given to the Groom
Traded to the Trucker
Punished by the Principal
Wifed by the Warlord

THE DRAGON'S CURVY MATE SERIES
Dragon's Curvy Assistant
Dragon's Curvy Banker
Dragon's Curvy Counselor
Dragon's Curvy Doctor
Dragon's Curvy Engineer
Dragon's Curvy Firefighter
Dragon's Curvy Gambler

THE CURVY IN COLLEGE SERIES
The Jock and the Genius
The Rockstar and the Recluse
The Dropout and the Debutante
The Player and the Princess
The Fratboy and the Feminist

WWW.ANNABELLEWINTERS.

Traded to the Trucker

By

Annabelle Winters

1
QUAKE

"**Q**uitting tonight," I grunt, glancing at the stupefied gas-station attendant as I slide a single cigarette out of the pack of filterless Winstons and then toss the other nineteen in the trash behind the counter. The kid's head is about the size of my palm, and he's got enough pimples to keep Clearasil in business for the next decade. Reminds me of how much I hated those years.

Of course, *these* years ain't that much better, I think as I dig for cash in my grease-stained Dickie's Dungarees which have more pockets than my truck has gears. I chuckle when my fingers kiss the stiff edge of a condom wrapper. Still intact. Fuck, how long has it been since I took my own private rig out for a spin? Maybe after I deliver this shipment I stop by Trucker's Paradise and drop off the other load I've been carrying around for the last thousand miles. I hear they got some nice clean girls there, and although I ain't never paid for it yet, right now I could use the release without having to worry about all the shit that comes with bringing a girl home with me. Too much to explain to any woman I want to keep as my own.

And a whole lot more I can't explain.

"Here you go," I say, finding a wad of bills in one of the cargo flaps and peeling off a hundred. I toss it onto the counter, raising an eyebrow at the kid. I don't know if he's never seen a hundred before or if he just assumes that a guy like me had to have killed someone to be carrying around a stack of C-notes in his dungarees.

And you know what?

He'd be right.

"Keep the change," I call to him as I grab the 2-liter bottle of Mountain Dew Red and the 3-pound bag of Teriyaki Jerky, stick the single cigarette between my rough sunburned lips, and stride out the door.

The night is starless and moonless and dark as

sin, and I amble around the corner to the air-pumping station to enjoy my solitary smoke. I stick the torpedo-shaped Mountain Dew Red under my arm and pat my dungarees looking for a matchbook. I find that condom again and sigh, shaking my head and staring at the clean white cigarette that I know is filthy like my soul, poison like the blood in my veins, foul like the dark heart that somehow keeps beating even though I ain't got much to live for.

"Give you a dollar for that cigarette," comes a voice. A woman's voice. Soft like a pillow. Sweet like a song. But there's a tremble hidden in there, and when I glance in her direction I'm struck like a gong in one of those Kung Fu movies.

Her hair is thick and wavy like fresh gunsmoke, with long, meandering locks that twist and turn their way down her broad shoulders and smooth neck like a river opening up into a delta as it meets the sea. Her eyes are dark brown like there's a shadow behind those pupils, and when she brings her black-painted fingertips to red glossy lips as she asks for my cigarette again, I shake my head and grin.

"I already put it in my mouth," I say. "You might catch something, honey."

She raises an eyebrow and lets her gaze ride up

and down, from my battered construction boots to my stained dungarees all the way up my ripped tank top that barely covers the scars that adorn my torso like artwork. Artwork that came with a price. More than anyone will ever know.

"Can't be any worse than what's already in that cigarette," she says with a shrug. She holds up the dollar bill and flicks her hair back. "We got a deal or what?"

I study the cigarette and touch my left eyebrow. "It's the only one I got," I say. "I'll share it with you. But on one condition."

"What's that?" she says, tilting her head just enough for the flickering neon sign to light up her face—and more than enough for me to see a thin scar along her left cheek. An old scar. A scar that I immediately know made its mark deeper than just the skin.

"That it's the last cigarette we ever smoke," I say, blinking as I force my attention away from that scar.

She snorts and then crosses her arms beneath her breasts, pushing them up in a way that makes me stiffen and shift as I realize that she's got some heavenly heft under that black-and-yellow blouse that's regrettably buttoned all the way up.

"The last cigarette *we* ever smoke?" she says, tapping her foot and scrunching her lip at the same time. "But we're two strangers meeting at a gas station on the highway. After tonight we'll never see each other again. How will we ever know if the other person kept their promise?"

"Sounds like someone ain't that good at keeping a promise," I say, pursing my lips. "That's disappointing."

She laughs, rubbing her arms as she shifts her weight from one hip to the other. I'm already hard just from talking to this chick, and I don't dare glance at those hips if I know what's good for me. I'm so hard up I'm already imagining tossing her into my monstrous truck-cab and showing her the back bench. I'd take her hard and fast, bent over double, ass up in the air for Daddy, thick thighs glistening with pussy juice as I ram my heavy piston deep into her slick cylinder. I'd cover her mouth when she comes, run my thick finger along that scar, make her come again before pulling out just in time to paint her asscrack and lower back with my thick semen. Then we'd share that cigarette, get back into our vehicles, and never see each other again.

"If you think *that's* disappointing, wait till you get to know me," she says, widening her eyes and then winking and clicking her tongue.

"I ain't got time to wait," I shoot back, licking

my burning lips and cracking a quicksilver smile. "Got to deliver my load before sunrise, and I never miss a deadline. I'll just have to trust you, honey. You got a light?"

"My mom used to call me honey," she says, reaching into her bag and pulling out a heavy bronze Zippo. She clinks the lid open and snaps her fingers, summoning the red-blue flame like a sorceress of the night. "She's dead now."

I breathe deep, taking in the smell of lighter fluid as I stick the cig between my lips and consider her words. I keep my eye on her as she saunters close, that flickering flame scorching the air between us, casting golden halos around our bodies as I lean in and let her light me up.

Even through the smoke I can smell her scent, and I breathe in her sweet essence along with the pungent tobacco. I take one long, deep drag and hand her the cigarette. She glances at the moist mark left by my lips, and then without hesitating puts her own lips right there, her brown eyes dancing in the trickster light of the starless night.

"So you don't keep promises," I say, reaching out and claiming the cigarette back before she smokes the entire thing. "And people who call you honey are dropping like flies." I glance at that scar and then blink when she notices. She touches her face almost unconsciously, and although I know the polite thing is to make no mention of it, I ain't much of a manners guy. So I take another puff, and as I hand the smoke back to her, I reach out and run my little finger along her scar, staring into her eyes as I do it, my jaw set tight, body coiled like a spring as electricity shoots through my sinews from the raw contact of skin on skin.

She flinches and slaps my hand away, but I see the bloodrush darken her cheeks and I know she felt that same spark. Fuck, I want to slide my big hand around the back of her neck, fist her thick brown hair as I taste those lips, kiss away the scars that she carries inside her, fuck her so hard it exorcises all her demons and maybe even mine.

"Asshole who did that is dead too, I hope," I say, shifting my gaze past her so she doesn't see what's behind my dark green eyes. I catch sight of the only other vehicle at the station, and I frown when I realize it's a silver Mercedes S-Class. That's a hundred-thousand dollar car, and I flick my eyes back to her face as my frown deepens.

And now paranoia runs through my icy veins, and I realize that I let my guard down. I've been running this route for years without any trouble, but I should know that the longer you run a route without trouble, the more likely it is that your next run is the one they catch you.

I glance down at her sensible shoes, rubbing the back of my neck as I hand back the cigarette and consider the possibility this chick is DEA or FBI or maybe even DHS. The car's a bit over-the-top for an undercover agent, but maybe that's the point.

"Asshole who did that is the love of my life and the father of my children," she says with a sly smile as she nods and accepts the smoldering cigarette's last drag. She sucks it down and then flicks it into the hedge.

I shake my head and stride over to the hedge, spreading the hardy shrubs so I can reach for the burning butt. I hold it up and shake my head again. "You know a gas station has thousands of gallons of gasoline in underground tanks, right? You looking to take out the entire county?"

At least I know she isn't the law, I decide when she cackles out a laugh as I douse the cigarette in a half-empty cup of congealed coffee that's sitting on the air-fill station box. I also know she's married with kids, and that's enough of a cue for me to be on my way. Yeah, it's tempting to dig deeper into that scar and why she's still with a guy who'd do that to her. But that sounds like drama, and I don't do drama. Besides, I've made enough questionable choices in my wretched life that it's fucking laughable for me to question someone else's choices.

"Nice knowing you," I grunt, picking up my drink and snack and squinting as a pair of headlights sweep across the deserted gas station. "My regards to the love of your life."

I pop the cap and take a deep swig of the caffeinated red drink that's my fuel when I'm under the gun to hit my delivery deadline. I can stay awake for three days straight on this shit—though I'm pretty sure I was hallucinating like a hippie the last time I did that. I glance at my G-Shock Chrono and grunt. It's only ten. I got a solid eight hours before the sun shows itself.

"He's a surgeon," she calls after me.

"What?" I say, half-turning as that other car circles the lot and then heads out without stopping for gas or anything else. Strange, but maybe they saw me in my grease-stained pants and torn muscle tank and assumed that if they stopped I'd rip them apart like chicken wings and eat them bones and all just for the hell of it.

"Husband's a surgeon," she says, smiling and blinking as she touches the scar and shrugs. "Removed a small growth in my jaw. It was nothing. Benign cyst."

I exhale and nod, smiling back even though I get the sense she isn't giving me the full story. Seems a pretty big scar for a small growth, but what the fuck do I know. I barely made it through high-school.

My silver-and-black semi-truck looms into view as the crickets call out from the weeds beyond the big-rig lot. I reach for my keys, chuckling when I feel that condom wrapper in my pocket. Still chuckling, I pull it out and squint at the date. Expired. I toss it onto the floormats and climb behind the wheel of my rig. Then I glance at my watch again, do a quick calculation of my ETA, and with a sigh reach for the GPS.

"Trucker's Paradise by 2 a.m.," I mutter as that silver Mercedes screeches out of the lot. I'm still hot and hard after sharing spit with that surgeon's wife, and maybe it's time I see if the rumors about the unmarked barrack-style building that the Syndicate owns down the way from Trucker's Paradise really is the cleanest little whorehouse this side of the Canadian border.

I pull my beast of a truck into the driveway leading to the on-ramp, and then I slam on the brakes when a black car whizzes past me. I'm about to lay on the horn, but the guy's gone. I wonder if it's the same car that did a circle of the gas station earlier, but there's no way to know. Still, that second car took off in the same direction as that woman's silver Benz. Shouldn't mean anything—after all, there's only two ways to turn on this part of the road. But things feel a little off, and if I were a better man maybe I'd . . .

"You'd what? Follow that surgeon's wife just to make sure she's OK? And what if she sees you and decides you're stalking her? What if she calls it in? You wanna get pulled over when you got a trailer full of shit that would get you locked up for life?"

No danger of spending too much time behind bars though, I think as my rig rumbles onto the highway and picks up steam like a locomotive heading downhill. Because the Syndicate would make sure that life sentence ended quickly, with me having a horrible "accident" involving a toothbrush, a sharpened dime, and a bar of soap.

And with that I switch off my imagination and turn on my driving lights. Just me and the road, baby. Alone on the road, just like my dream. The only dream I have these days.

2
QUINNIE

Am I dreaming or did that trucker smell clean like soap?

I keep one hand on the wheel and try to keep one eye on the road as I tap the multicolored dashboard screen and try to figure out how to get a radio station that isn't hillbilly talk. I'm startled by a whirring sound, and I curse out loud when I realize I just opened the darned moonroof.

The cool night air swirls in like a snake, and I curse again and try to pull the moonroof closed. But like everything in this fancy new car you have to control it through the computer, and finally I give up and try to be grateful that it's late summer and still reasonably warm, even though we're pretty far north, less than a hundred miles from the Canadian border.

"Now what?!" I yell when that dratted dashboard lights up again. But this time a picture pops up. That smiling photo of Richard taken a decade ago, a year after we got married on the Ritz Carlton's rooftop in Chicago, Lake Michigan looking sleek and shiny, black as sin under a moonless night.

Somehow I manage to answer the call, and when Richard's nasally loud voice fills the Blaupunkt speakers and almost gives me an instant migraine, I grip the wheel tight and swallow hard so I don't groan out loud.

"What?" I say, squinting as two bright white LED headlamps pull up close behind me, sending blinding reflections into my eyes from the rearview mirror. I'm about to honk at the guy, but it's dumb to honk at someone who's behind you. What the fuck is he doing kissing my bumper like that?

"Just checking in," says Richard in that nasal voice that's cold like the shady pond on our Lake Forest property that never gets any sun. "Where are you? Oh. Never mind. I see you."

I frown at the screen, tilting my head and wondering if that's him in the car behind me. Which is ridiculous, of course. Richard's five hundred miles away in Chicago. "Oh no," I deadpan. "Did you die and now your ghost is haunting me?"

Richard doesn't get the joke. Richard never gets the joke. Surgically precise like a scalpel. Cold and controlled both inside and outside. In ten years I haven't seen him cry, haven't heard him laugh, haven't got much evidence that he's not just a ghost who sleeps in my bed and fucks me a couple of times a year with all the lights off and the curtains drawn like he can't bear to look at my body. I assumed he imagines someone else, and although that might hurt another woman's ego, I don't care.

Because I imagine someone else too.

Not anyone I actually know, of course. Just someone who isn't Richard. Someone who doesn't spend all his free time grooming himself like a serial killer. I swear I've seen him shave his arms all the way up to the elbow because he worries about infecting a patient during surgery!

I caress my scar, my toes curling as I remember how that mean-looking trucker ran his little finger along my face in a way that made my butt tighten, made my pussy clench, made me a little bit wet in my panties. Hell, he got me more turned on with one stroke of his pinky finger than Richard has in ten years with his cock. I don't even *remember* the last time Richard made me come, and for the past three years I've lost interest to the point where I don't even bother making myself come.

"Your new car has a GPS tracker that links to an app on my phone," Richard announces. "Can't be too careful these days. Why'd you stop at that gas station for so long, anyway?"

I glare at the screen, not sure if I should be furious or amused. Of*course* Richard's birthday gift to me came with some way for him to stay in control. I wouldn't be surprised if he can just take over the steering wheel from his phone. Maybe he'd drive me straight through the railing, into that dark river that I noticed snaking its way back and forth below the highway like it's stalking me.

"You timed my visit to the gas station?" I say, relaxing a bit as that annoying car drops back and dips its headlamps. "How long was I there?"

"Twenty six minutes," Richard says cordially, like he's reading it off a log he keeps. "What were you doing?"

"Cheating on you, of course," I say with a casual shrug and a rueful smile because I know he'd never believe it. "How about you? How's that nurse you're banging in the broom closet at the hospital?" I'm totally messing with him, of course. "Tell her I said hi."

Richard's silence is so fierce I can almost hear it crackle through the speakers. I don't know why I just said that. Maybe I'm just slap-happy after that strangely liberating cigarette I shared with that beast of a trucker back at the gas station. Maybe somewhere in the back of my mind I let myself think of what a braver, wilder woman would have done back there . . . would have let that trucker do to her back there.

But I'm not a cheater, and I'm darned sure Richard isn't either. If he were cheating on me, he'd fuck me more than twice a year. Cheating husbands always fuck their wives a little more, a little harder, a little deeper. I should know. My first husband was a cheater.

And I wish David had been not just my first but my last husband too, I think as Richard finally recovers enough to force a bloodless chuckle at my feisty little jab that a more self-confident man would have found super funny. And David would have been my last husband if I hadn't gotten screwed by signing that pre-nup without getting my own lawyer. I was a twenty-something in love (or so I thought . . .) back then, and when David told me the pre-nup was a standard thing required by the investors in his start-up, I shrugged and signed and skipped my way down the aisle like an airhead who had no idea how the world worked, how marriage worked, how love worked.

And how love *didn't* work.

"Don't work too hard while I'm gone," I say softly as Richard clears his throat like he's trying to think of something to say after my off-the-cuff comment about both of us cheating on each other. For a moment I get the eerie sense that maybe we'd both be relieved if the other one was cheating. Maybe it would give us a way out of this marriage that got the seven-year itch after eighteen months and is now like a rash that won't go away.

"Quinnie, listen," Richard says after clearing his throat again. Immediately I stiffen, sensing that we're finally getting to the point of this call. Richard doesn't just call to "check in" on me. He never does anything without a clear agenda, a rehearsed script, an objective that can be summarized in three bullet-points.

"What's up," I say cheerfully, sighing when I see that black car move close again. I wonder if I've slowed down, but I'm still humming along at ten over the speed limit. I lean on the gas a bit, feeling the powerful engine open up as I pull ahead. Then I get back to Richard's scripted agenda.

"I'm sorry," Richard finally says. "I'm sorry it didn't work out for us, Quinnie."

I frown as his words bounce around in my head before finally lodging themselves in my brain like a surgical probe. I shake my head a few times like I'm trying to rattle something loose, and then I glance at his smiling photograph as the sudden realization hits me that this is a *divorce* conversation! Richard planned this entire thing—from gifting me the car to suggesting I drive to Wyoming for a luxury spa getaway—so he could have this conversation when I'm five hundred miles away! The little shit redefines the term "non-confrontational!"

My mind spins through the scenario lightning quick, and I swallow hard when a sudden flash of elation rips through me. Like any woman in a loveless marriage, I've fantasized about what changes a divorce might bring. And like any woman married to a millionaire, I've run the numbers too.

Of course, Richard asked me to sign a pre-nup back then too. I agreed, but this time I hired my own lawyer to look it over. It was precise and concise, clean and neat, just like everything Richard did. The only scenario where I'd get nothing in a divorce would be if I cheated on him. In pretty much every other situation, it would be a seventy-thirty split—which I agreed to since I didn't have much to my name when we got married and Richard was already earning in the high six figures at the time.

"Um, can this conversation wait until I get back, Richard?" I say finally, pushing away thoughts of freedom that make me want to shake my butt and scream out the window like a wild she-beast who just broke out of the zoo.

"It's not a conversation," Richard says. "It's a farewell. Goodbye, Quinnie."

"What?" I say, frowning as that car behind me snaps on its highbeams again, blinding me for a moment and making me swerve into the right lane. Somehow I manage to not slam into the guardrail past the shoulder, but when I regain control my heart is thumping like someone's in there trying to kick their way out.

And just as Richard's words sink in, just as I realize that I'm an idiot, that I've done it again, gotten married for the wrong reasons, chosen the wrong man, picked the wrong path in life, I see that big black car roar towards me from behind.

The car rams into my bumper so hard my teeth rattle in my head. I scream and swerve as I try to accelerate away. But although my car is fast, the beastly black car is bigger and more powerful, and it rams into my rear again and again until I realize the highway's bending and I'm about to be pushed through the guardrail and get launched like a kite over the dark, winding river!

There's no time to think, breathe, or even fucking scream. But somehow I do all those things at once, and with a holy howl I *slam* my foot on the brake, *yank* the parking-brake up at the same time, and then scream again as the black car slams so hard into me that it flips over on its side as I spin like a top.

The black car rolls three times and lands right side up, but I'm still spinning like the teacup ride at Disneyworld, and as I stare at the looming darkness beyond the silver guardrail that's getting bigger and bigger, I know there's nothing more I can do. Everything in my life has led me to this point, it occurs to me as a lazy smile spreads on my face. I don't even want to blame Richard. After all, I married him for the wrong reasons.

"I married for money," I whisper, a shiver going through me as I finally admit it out loud, admit that I'm a gold-digger, a woman who decided that love had no place in marriage, that marriage was an economic alliance and the economics were fucking good with Richard even if everything else was awful. I chose money over love, the mind over the heart, the material over the spiritual. I made the leap ten years ago with my eyes wide open, and now I'm paying the price.

And just as I finish the thought I slam into the guardrail with an unholy screech of metal on metal. Sparks fly and steel snaps, and then suddenly there's a bang and a flash and everything goes dark, full dark, forever dark.

3
QUAKE

I'm in a dark mood by the time the pink neon of Trucker's Paradise flickers through the black trees that line the highway. My mind's been stuck on that woman I met at the gas station, and I lick my dry lips again, yearning to get a taste of that candied mouth, get a whiff of that feminine scent, catch another glimpse of her wide hips as she walks away from me.

"Quake, you're a fucking idiot!" I shout, turning my wheel hard when the exit comes up sooner than I expect. I feel my load swing wildly behind me, but I'm not going to tip her. I may be an idiot, but I know how to handle my rig even in an icestorm.

My problem is that I can't handle anything else in this lonely shitshow that's my life.

I park the rig and circle round back to make sure my load's secure. I test the electronic padlock and grunt. I don't have the passcode for the lock. I never have the passcode for the lock. I don't know what's inside, and I sure as hell don't *wanna* know what's inside. Shit, in ten years of being a delivery guy I've probably carried every kind of contraband under the moon and stars: Drugs, guns, and everything in between. Except people, of course. I know some runners handle "live" loads across the borders, but that's where I draw the line. I ain't no saint when it comes to the oldest profession in the world; but if a girl wants to sell her body, it should be her own fucking choice, not someone else's.

"And there's plenty of ways to sell your body," I mutter, slapping the swinging padlock and stretching my arms out wide. I run my big hands over my short-cropped hair that's always military style even though I flamed out of the Marines after barely making it eighteen months. I grin tightly as I push away the memories of those lost years after I somehow managed to get an honorable discharge and thought I'd dodged a bullet only to stumble into a marriage that cleaned me out in more ways than one, broke my bank account and also my . . . heart?

Nah, I think with a snort. She didn't break my heart because I never really loved her. What she broke was my faith. Faith in women. And in myself, I suppose. But mostly women.

The distant sound of high-pitched laughter comes to me along with the sawthroated guitar riff of an 80's rock song. I sniff the air and can almost taste the tequila, smell the sensimilla. We're a long ways from Mexico, but it's the same guys that run this entire corridor—from border to border: Canada to Mexico. Borders are way less policed up north, and it turns out the Canadians have their dark, ugly habits too, just like the rest of us.

I pocket my keys and check my cash, cracking my knuckles and swinging my arms to loosen my back muscles. I feel my shoulder blades catch, and I wince and move my neck until I finally get my range of motion all set. A ripple of energy goes through me, and I clench and release my fists like I'm aching for some excuse to get the blood hot and pumping.

"Well, that's what Trucker's Paradise specializes in," I say as I walk past the main truck-stop, keeping my head low as I beeline to the unmarked brown building that's almost rocking on its foundation from what's going on inside.

Two beer-bellied long-haulers tumble out the steel front door, one of them with his belt still undone, both of them red in the face and panting. I avert my eyes as they walk past in a cloud of stogie-smoke and coffee-vapors. The stench makes my stomach curdle, and by the time I get to the whorehouse steps I'm almost doubled over with what feels like what grandpa used to call the heebie-jeebies.

"I can't fucking do this," I realize, straightening up and almost laughing at myself. I've stared into loaded guns more times than I can count, fought my way into and out of life-and-death situations like it's my job, walked away from accidents that would've broken the hardest of men. But I'm scared shitless on the front steps of a whorehouse like a teenager who's never seen tits that weren't on a computer screen, never smelled a clean, wet pussy, never tasted that sweet nectar that calls to your cock like a siren singing your tune.

It's that surgeon's wife, I decide as I turn on my heel and hurry back toward my truck like I need to get outta here before I change my mind. But just as I make it to the grass triangle so I can cut across to my rig, a banged up black car careens into the lot and squeaks towards the back side of the whorehouse. I frown as I think about that black car I saw earlier. The same one? Hard to tell, especially since this guy has two busted headlights and ugly dents all over like the sonofabitch got flipped like a pancake and rolled like a pastry.

I rub my jaw as I stand beneath a tree in that triangle of dark grass. I should mind my own business, especially since I'm carrying a full load and I got a deadline coming up. But something tells me this black car *is* my business. Maybe it's that restless energy I felt when I cracked my knuckles and opened up my back. Maybe it's because that surgeon's wife got me all hard and horny and I need an outlet for that energy. Maybe since I chose to avoid the sex I'm aching for some violence to clear my head.

By the time I'm done spinning through why this is a bad fucking idea, I'm already at the side wall of the whorehouse, staying in the shadows of the second-floor overhang as I make my way around to the back. I stop when I see the black car pulled up against a dumpster at the far end of the lot. Then I hold my breath and try to merge into the wall when two guys stride out of the whorehouse, both of them with shoulder holsters over their black shirts like this is the wild west or something.

The armed men pass beneath a lamppost, and I silently curse when I see the telltale tattoos on the back of their shaved heads. I know those tattoos. I've known those tattoos for years. If I weren't an independent contractor, I'd have one of those on my own thick neck. These guys are BSG—Border Syndicate Group. Sometimes called BS for short—though this gang is far from BS. They're legit, and I should know: I run goods for the same Syndicate. That's their load on my trailer, in fact.

Two guys climb out of the black car, and from the way they groan and stagger I can tell they're hurt. Definitely been in an accident, and from the looks of it I bet they're gonna need some medical attention. This isn't the place for it, though. So why are they here?

"Ran into a problem on an off-the-books job," says the first guy from the black car. He's got unwashed red hair with dark streaks of what looks like dried blood. "Need to stash her here so I can get my buddy to the hospital. He's hurt real bad, coughing up blood. Gotta get myself checked out too. Hit my head. Think I broke my arm. And my neck don't work right."

"Your brain don't work right either," says Syndicate-Thug, who glances into the backseat and then jerks his head back and spits out an undecipherable curse. "Who the fuck is she?"

"Some doctor's wife," says Blackcar-Thug. "We was supposed to ram her off the road above the river valley."

"So why's she still alive? More importantly, why the fuck is she *here*?"

Blackcar-Thug rubs his left eye that isn't tracking straight. "Coz she was supposed to go into the river in her car. But we got in an accident, and her car won't start."

"So just push the fucking car over the edge," grunts Syndicate-Thug.

Blackcar-Thug runs his hand through his hair and exhales hard. "She didn't hit the guardrail clean enough to break the steel barrier. We was gonna just toss her over, but the guy specifically wanted her to go over in the car. Guess he wanted it to look like an accident."

Syndicate-Thug touches his gun and then rubs his smooth brown face. Obviously Blackcar-Thug isn't thinking clearly after the accident, and Syndicate-Thug isn't paid to be a thinker. This is the blind leading the blind, which means that the one-eyed man is king.

So I close one eye and step out of the shadows, holding my arms out wide and my head up high. I take slow, measured steps as the Syndicate thugs draw their weapons.

"I work for BSG," I say in a colorless monotone. "That's my silver rig in the other lot. You can check the load—trailer's got a Syndicate electronic padlock with the insignia."

Syndicate-Thug keeps his gun on me as he glances at my rig in the distance. Then he studies my face, and although he isn't a thinker, he's got enough instinct to sense I'm not stupid enough to lie about something that would take two seconds to verify. He grunts and lowers his weapon, nodding once at his buddy before turning back to me.

"All right. So what?" he says. "You looking for the company discount, Trucker?"

I shrug and force a sideways grin. I'm not much of a thinker either, but I got some instinct that's served me well. I also have big fucking balls, and that's what I need if I'm gonna pull this off.

"Looking to make a trade," I drawl, licking my lips and nodding my head at the busted black car. "I heard him say things got fucked up, and since I been doing business with BSG going on a decade now, I thought I'd offer my services. I got a proposition that'll make everyone real happy. A trade that'll work real nice. Everyone gets what they want." I rub my jaw, shrug, and flash a wicked grin that feels real in a way I didn't expect. "Except the good doctor's wife, of course. Give her to me for a few hours. I'll clean up your mess, use her till sunrise, and then toss her in the river-valley before the roosters sound the call."

4
QUINNIE

"Why do I hear roosters in my head," I mutter as I stare out the tinted window of what appears to be the back bench of an empty semi-truck cab. It's dark outside, and the night's cooled down enough that there's a wispy layer of fog crawling through the air like ghostly spiders.

I groan and try to scratch my nose, but my hands are tied and so I just scrunch up my face. My cheeks and lips and eyelids are all raw and itchy, almost like I got sunburned. Now I remember that airbag exploding in my face when I crashed, and I decide that a tender face is a small price to pay for not being dead. Now what do I have to give to not be tied up?

My head pounds, but I feel mostly all right. Nothing feels broken, though I expect that to change pretty darned soon. Truth is, I don't know why I'm still alive. After all, Richard is precise and calculating even when we're planning a trip to the mall, and this plan feels kinda sloppy.

"I expected better, my love," I whisper sweetly as I lean my head against the window and sigh. The cab smells vaguely comforting, in a manly sort of way—like peppered beef jerky with a hint of cigarette smoke. There's also something else in the air—something clean but musky. Like a man's soap—which seems odd for a truck.

"Or a trucker," I gasp when the fog clears just enough to see movement outside. It's my car, I realize. And there's a man pushing it. A man who looks familiar!

I stare like a fish from a bowl as my cigarette-buddy trucker adjusts the positions of his baseball-glove sized hands on my Benz's bumper, tightens his triceps that are thicker than my thighs, digs his legs into the tarmac, and with a breathtaking flex of his powerful haunches pushes my brand new car right through a gap in the rail, sending it off into the foggy river-valley like blowing a feather into the breeze.

He grunts and stretches his arms out wide before stepping to the edge of the road and peering over. It must be a long ways down, because I don't hear shit. But then I realize I'm behind the thick glass of a truck cab, and I almost smile before the panic finally hits me like it's been waiting for its chance.

I'm hyperventilating by the time the trucker yanks open the driver-side door and clambers in, and when he sees I'm awake he grins and leans in between the seats, his broad body blocking out pretty much all the light from the above-dash bulb.

"Your husband wanted you to go over with that car," he says.

"Tell me something I don't know," I say.

The trucker taps his lower lip and raises his left eyebrow. "Let's see . . . ah, here's something." He focuses his eyes on me, and I notice they're deep green like an exotic ocean, piercing like spears, bright like lanterns. "I promised some guys that your husband was gonna get what he wanted before sunrise."

The panic's still got me by the throat, but somehow I remember a snippet of our conversation earlier in the night. "You accused me of not being a promise-keeper. I sure as hell hope you suck at keeping promises too."

The trucker grins and shakes his head. The smile is real, and for a fraction of a second the man looks less like a murderous thug and more like . . . well, like the man I shared a naughty smoke with not so long ago. Shared some spit too, I think as I glance at his rough lips and swallow hard when I recall how I tasted him on that secret cigarette we shared.

He slides into his seat and adjusts the center mirror so he can see me dead on. "We're lucky no one noticed your busted up Benz and called the cops," he says, totally avoiding my question about whether he's going to keep his promise about tossing me after my poor car before sunrise.

I hold up my twist-tied hands and wiggle my fingers. "Lucky isn't a word I'd use to describe my situation, thanks very much."

"You're welcome," he grunts, punching the ignition switch with a thumb bigger than my fist. The truck roars to life, and I feel the vibrations so deep it's like I'm in one of those massage chairs.

Now I think about the spa trip that Richard sent me on, and I almost throw up as a potent mixture of red rage and black despair squeezes my insides until I gasp for air.

"You all right?" he calls over the rumble of the engine. Those green eyes seek me out in the mirror, and again I get a glimpse of the man inside the beast, a man who's got some darkness back there but isn't all dark.

At least I hope he isn't all dark.

"What the fuck do you think?" I snap at him, slumping down against the smooth fake leather of the back bench and pouting. "My husband just tried to have me killed, and now I'm tied up in the backseat of a truck. Why am I tied up, anyway? What the hell is going on? What are you going to do with me?"

And what are you going to do TO me, I think as I catch those green eyes shoot a look at my cleavage, which has a nice bruise square in the center.

"Don't know yet," he says, glancing at the sideview mirror as he pulls the rig off the shoulder and onto the road.

"When *will* you know?"

He frowns at me, and his eyes narrow just enough to let me know he's stifling a smile. "You always ask so many questions?"

"You always answer every question with another question?"

The trucker chuckles, his massive body shaking as his eyes light up. He pulls off at the next exit and takes the overpass across the highway. I figure he needs to head the other direction. There's a small mom-and-pop gas station on the left, and I get a flash of hope, like maybe I could get them to call the cops on this guy and save my hog-tied ass before my skydiving date at sunrise.

"I gotta pee," I say. "Stop at the gas station."

The trucker snorts and makes the turn onto the highway without even slowing down. "There's an unmanned rest stop forty miles up."

"I can't hold it that long."

"Then you can go in the bushes up ahead. I may not be the sharpest pea in the pod, but I ain't *that* dumb."

I raise an eyebrow and glance at his eyes. "Did you just say the *sharpest* pea in the pod?"

He blinks, and even in the dim glow of the dashboard lights I see him turn dark with color. He rubs his jaw and tightens his grip on the thick steering wheel until I almost hear it groan like it's gonna crumble to powder if he doesn't ease up.

"You ain't that bright yourself if you think making fun of me is a good idea," he mutters through a sulky scowl.

I sigh and tug on my twist-ties. "No, I'm probably not that bright, considering I didn't see this coming. Didn't think Richard was capable of something like this."

"Richard's your husband? The doctor?" He pauses, darting a look at me as I nod. "You love him?"

"Probably not the best time to ask me that question."

We drive in silence for a while, and the trucker reaches for the bag of jerky. He rips it open with his teeth, and without turning offers me some. I sigh and maneuver my tied hands so I can pick out a strip. "Thanks," I say softly, tearing off a chunk with my teeth and almost moaning when the salty goodness lights me up like it's Christmas. "My name's Quinnie, by the way."

The trucker takes his bag of jerky back and pushes a handful of the dried beef into his gaping maws. I wait for him to say something, but he just chews and swallows and takes a gulp from a two-liter bottle of red soda.

"You don't talk much," I say, pushing away the bag when he offers me some more.

"Can't talk and think at the same time."

I sigh and wince, wondering if it would be easier if he just killed me now so I don't have to go through the pain of this conversation. "OK. So what are you thinking about?"

He sighs. "Well, now that you got me talking, I ain't thinking about shit."

"Great," I say cheerfully. "So what's your name?"

"What difference does it make?"

"Why are you so pissed off? I'm the one tied up with a fucking death contract on my head!"

The trucker rumbles air out past his lips like a second-grader. "Quake," he says gruffly.

I frown. "Quake? What's that?"

"You asked my name. It's Quake. Are we done talking now?"

"Quake," I say, feeling my lips pucker up as I say the word. "Quake."

"Ma said I was born during an earthquake," he says stiffly, rubbing the back of his neck and shifting in his seat. He glances back at me and winks. "She's dead now," he whispers, playing my own words from earlier back to me almost like we're flirting in the darkest possible way.

I reward him with a smile, and for a moment I almost relax as the heavy truck rumbles down the black road, the thick of night hugging us like a blanket. Again thoughts of Richard threaten to squeeze my insides to pulp, but I push them away and force myself to focus on the here and now, on what's in front of me.

"You saved my life, didn't you?" I say suddenly as I put together the snippets of information I picked up from this monosyllabic monolith of a man.

He grunts and shrugs, casting another look at

me in the mirror and then rubbing his jaw that's the size and shape of an old-style streetlamp. "Not exactly. Postponed your death is more like it."

I bite my lip and stare at the back of Quake's head. Military style buzzcut. Shoulders broader than the Golden Gate Bridge. Biceps thicker than my thighs. Palms big enough to crush a man's head like a grape.

"You ever killed someone before, Quake?" I say, doing my best to keep my voice steady.

Those green eyes darken, but Quake doesn't even flinch. "What do you think?"

I stare at him as I decide. "Nobody who didn't deserve it," I say softly, not sure why I know that. Maybe it's just blind hope, a desperate need to believe that Quake isn't all bad, that if he postponed my death so he can figure out the next step, maybe I need to help him figure it out. Besides, what choice do I have? The man who vowed to love me forever just paid a couple of goons to push me off a cliff. But Quake's been up front that killing me is still an option—which, given my history, makes him the most honest man I've ever met!

"I've had to defend myself a couple of times when some rival gang tried to jack my load," he says. "Used to do hits for the Syndicate, but stopped taking those jobs."

"Why'd you stop?"

He shrugs. "Didn't need the extra money. Paid off all the debt my ex saddled me with. Don't spend a lot, and I don't need a lot. Two or three runs a year is enough to keep me cruising."

"So you work a few weeks a year? What do you do in your spare time? You got kids with your ex?"

Quake shakes his head and then whistles like he dodged a bullet. "You got kids, right?"

I smile. "No. I just said that earlier because . . ." I touch my lip and glance furtively at him. "Because I thought you were hitting on me. Most guys don't have a problem with a married woman. But tell a guy you have kids and he backs off."

Quake glares at me in the mirror, and I see his fingers tighten around the wheel again. "If I were hitting on you," he says with a quiet confidence that makes my toes curl, "I wouldn't have backed off. Not even if your husband and kids were right there with you. Trust me, honey. If I decided you were mine, I'd have made you mine."

I gasp at his directness, and I swear I feel my thighs tighten as my pussy releases a whisper of wetness into my pink satin panties. I sense him looking into that broad mirror that's pointed right at my big boobs, and my pussy clenches like it's swallowing as I imagine this beast of a man swatting Richard aside and then claiming me face-down right on the Thanksgiving table, with Richard's stodgy old-world parents squealing and bleating and fanning themselves as I snort like a mare in heat while Quake stuffs me fuller than the turkey bouncing right next to our sweaty bodies.

The fantasy almost makes me laugh, and as Quake focuses on the road to maneuver around a slowpoke U-haul van, the fantasy merges with reality to create a strange landscape that's part nightmare, part dream. That hot rage I'd felt earlier is now a cold hatred for Richard, and the only heat I'm feeling is between my legs, like this whole near-death experience has flipped everything on its head, like I no longer give a damn about anything, that there's no point following society's rules and morals and laws if you can do all that and still end up marrying a lizard like Richard.

"You said sunrise," I say, running my tongue over my lip as I think aloud. "But we've got longer than that before anyone can be sure I didn't go over the cliff with my car. After all, I could've been thrown clear, rolled far from the wreckage, maybe even gotten swept away downriver. Richard wouldn't be sure I was alive, and neither would the guys with whom you made the trade." I raise my chin and frown. "Which was what, by the way?"

"The trade?" His eyes widen as he shifts and

clears his throat. "Well," he says, clearing his throat again and glancing at my cleavage before hurriedly looking away. "I said I'd finish what those thugs started, and in return I'd get . . ." He swallows and shifts again, and I firm my lower lip and sit up straight, totally enjoying watching this monster of a man squirm as I force him to admit what I can already guess.

"You'd get me," I say firmly, my buttocks tightening as my pussy squeezes out a little more of my secret wetness. "You'd get me until sunrise. Turn me into a sex doll for a couple of hours before tossing me off a cliff like yesterday's garbage. You guys are sick."

Quake grins and shrugs like a kid who just got caught fingering the cookie jar. "Hey, I had to tell them something believable. I could've asked for money, but they'd know I get paid well for running goods for the Syndicate."

"My point still stands: You guys are sick. All of you. Everyone from Richard on down. Just a bunch of twisted animals who chew on dried meat and use women like playthings."

Quake glances at the half-empty bag of jerky and frowns over at me. "Careful," he says in a soft growly voice that makes me want to purr. "Once

I'm done with my dried meat, I might get a hankering for play."

I roll my eyes, for some reason not threatened even though I'm completely at Quake's mercy. It's almost surreal, but I guess if Quake wanted to turn me into a sex doll, he's already had plenty of opportunity. I was right about him. He's not *all* dark.

But hopefully he's dark enough, I think as our eyes meet in the quicksilver of the mirror. Dark enough for what I'm about to propose.

5
QUAKE

"You want to hire me to kill your husband," I say, the words coming out slowly like I'm giving her every chance to correct me, to tell me I heard wrong, that she spoke wrong, that all of this is wrong. "Listen, honey. You're in no position to be hiring anyone to do anything."

"Fine," she says, that pretty round face looking seductive and mysterious in the dull glow of the truck's interior lights. "What's *your* idea, genius? We both know you aren't going to toss me off a cliff."

I glower at the *genius* jab, responding by narrowing my eyes to wolf-like slits and making her blink. "I still might," I growl.

"Sure," she says, dismissing my growl with an eye-roll as I try to hide my amazement that even tied up and trapped this woman has a self-assured confidence that's hot as hell. Richard must be the dumbest surgeon East of the Mississippi. Hell, I should kill him just to make the world a smarter place! "Look," she continues. "You wouldn't have saved me if you were just gonna kill me anyway. But we both know you can't let me go either."

"Maybe I just keep you," I say, the words coming out before I can stop them. But they're out there, and they didn't come from that place where I made those jokes earlier. Because this wasn't a joke. This felt real.

Maybe I just keep her.

Keep her safe.

Keep her warm.

Keep her as mine.

I almost swerve off the road as raw emotion bubbles up in me so quick I lose vision for a moment. And in that moment I *see* a vision: It's me and Quinnie riding away on an endless highway through the clouds, a freeway to forever. It's an image so vivid I almost lose my mind, and when I manage to bring myself back to the road, I bring something back with me:

A decision.

A decision to keep her.

I glance at her reflection, wondering if she heard me . . . if she *felt* me. Instantly I know she did, and in those brown eyes I see something that makes me smile inside. I think back to that first meeting a few hours ago. Just two nameless strangers sharing a cigarette in the dark. Two strangers who shared the intimacy of a kiss in that moment. Two strangers who were connected by chance and are now connected by choice: My choice to save her.

And my choice to keep her.

"Where's that rest stop?" she says after a few miles and a few minutes and zero talk. The air is thick with tension, my words still hanging out there like smoke on a winter's night.

"Passed it ten miles ago," I say, keeping my eyes on the road as my cock stiffens from thoughts that would make a sex-doll blush. "Nothing more for another hour, at least." I scan my mirrors. No lights in sight. No traffic this far north at four in the morning. I glance over at the thick forest lining both sides of the highway. "I can stop on the shoulder. There's no one around for a hundred miles in every direction."

It takes her a moment to get what I'm suggesting. When she does her eyes almost pop out and bounce away. "I'll hold it," she says, a bit of color rushing to her healthy cheeks as she averts her eyes and slumps against the seatback.

But three minutes later she sighs and shakes her head. "All right. Pull over. But if a bear eats me while I'm peeing, my ghost is coming back to haunt your ass."

I chuckle as I pull the rig over to the shoulder and kill the engine. I reach for the hunting knife I tuck into the driver's side door, and when I turn to her she recoils.

"Relax," I say, touching her fingers and then holding her hands steady as I snip the plastic ties off with the knife edge that I bet is sharper than her asshole husband's surgical tools. "There. Now you can fight the bears yourself. Don't be long now."

"You aren't coming?" she says, rubbing her wrists and stealing a glance at me.

"I don't gotta go," I say, distracted by my burner flip phone that just buzzed. It's probably the 4 a.m. message from the Syndicate giving me the truck-bay number for my trailer-drop. "What?" I say when I realize she's still here. She doesn't reply, and I snort and shake my head. "You want me to stand watch for bears? Is that it?"

Quinnie shrugs, looks away, and then nods. "Maybe they'll recognize you as one of their own and leave me alone."

"Oh, yeah, now I remember—you're a fancy city girl. A surgeon's wife," I grumble as we dismount and head towards the thick treeline that's mostly Spruce and Douglas Fir up here. "And I'm just the grunt who'll fight a grizzly so you don't get your ass mauled. You know that if a bear does show up, I'm not gonna be that much help."

"Just speak to it in bear language," she calls from behind a thicket, her voice muffled by trees the size of my truck.

"One more wisecrack about me being a bear and I leave you here for the wolves," I call over my shoulder.

"Ohmygod, there are *wolves* here too?" she shrieks.

I shake my head and sigh, stretching my arms out wide and arching my back. I suck in a breath, savoring the oiled scent of the pines and the firs, the spice of the spruce, the faint smell of animal fur. Not a bear or a wolf, I think with a grin. Those beasts smell stronger than whiskey. This is probably a jackrabbit.

I hear the creature dart through the bushes, and I exhale and pull in another long breath, doing my best to ignore the distant tinkle of the surgeon's wife getting close to nature. She must have really needed to go. Why else would she put herself in such a vulnerable position, squatting like a village-girl, surrounded by wolves and bears, nothing but a curtain of leaves separating me from her.

Again it occurs to me that she feels safe in my presence, and again I think about that chance meeting earlier. Funny how fate works, ain't it? If we hadn't met, I probably wouldn't have interfered. Hell, I probably wouldn't even have driven to Trucker's Paradise if I hadn't gotten worked up like a dog in heat by that mysterious stranger who smelled like sin and tasted even better.

"You done?" I say, raising an eyebrow when I don't hear anything. I listen for the sound of Quinnie pulling her panties back up, and I wonder what color they are. I like red panties on a girl, but I bet the surgeon's wife wears plain beige like a good girl, a well-behaved woman.

My cock throbs as my filthy mind imagines her

wet pubic hairs pressing into the satin of her panties. Fuck, she'd smell so dirty and hot I've got half a mind to bust through those bushes and make her mine under the stars, show those big bad bears how it's done, make that alpha wolf howl for his mate when he smells my seed in the air.

"Quinnie? You all right?" I shift on my feet and turn, squinting as I scan for movement. It's too quiet, and finally I stride over to the thicket, pushing through with my muscular thighs.

And Quinnie's gone.

I stiffen like a soldier before an ambush, closing my eyes and processing every sound of the forest, every scent of the woods. Immediately I pick up her musk in the air, and I know she's hiding somewhere close, waiting for a chance to make a run for it.

"Don't be an idiot, Quinnie," I growl, clenching my fists as my blood rises. I don't like being tricked, and Quinnie is gonna learn that real quick. "I don't got time for games. I got a deadline for a drop, and the longer this goes on, the worse it's gonna—"

And now Quinnie makes a run for it, crashing out from a clump of spruce saplings to my left. I'm after her like a jaguar chasing an antelope, my hard, thick body smashing through anything smaller than a tree, my construction boots crushing roots and branches and any unlucky critter that's taking a nap in my path.

I see her weaving through the trees on my left, and I'm surprised when I catch a starlit glimpse of the ultra-focused look in her dark brown eyes. I keep pace with her, my long strides easily matching hers as I wait for a clearing so I can tackle her. But then she abruptly cuts left, and I lose sight of her for a moment before I realize she's made a U-turn and is doubling back to the truck!

"Fuck!" I roar, stumbling over an exposed root as I try to stop my heavy body's momentum so I can turn. Now I understand why she wanted me out of the truck, and I feel even dumber as my rage makes it hard to see . . .

. . . so hard to see that I get blindsided by a well-placed swing of a dead tree branch that catches me off balance and drops me hard to the forest floor!

It takes me a moment to realize I've been clubbed by Quinnie, and when I get back on my feet I'm seeing red stars everywhere, my blood boiling like hot oil, my fists clenched like sledgehammers. And my mood doesn't improve when I hear a door slam and then feel the full-throated roar of my rig coming to life.

But as fearless as this crazy chick might be,

no way she understands how an old-school double-clutch system works, and when I hear my beloved rig screech in protest as she tries to force it into the wrong gear, I howl and leap through the air, landing on the metal runner along the passenger side.

Quinnie screams as I punch through the window, shattering the thick glass with one blow. She tries to scramble out of the cab, but I drive myself through the broken window and grab her by the waistband of her jeans, yanking her back into the truck.

She kicks out at me with both feet, and I quickly realize those thighs of hers can throw some thunder. She gets me solid on the nose with her heel, busting it open so by the time I grab her ankles I'm snorting blood and seeing double. My head is throbbing like a group of amateur drummers inside my skull, and I shout like a madman as I finally bring this wild animal of a woman under control.

"You gonna learn to never do that again!" I roar, pressing her face-down into the seat and spreading her legs so I can jam my body in there to stop her from kicking my darned nose in again. I'm wild with adrenaline, burning with rage, boiling with heat, and in one quick motion I rip her jeans open down the back seam, tearing them down past her thighs.

Those pink panties come off like wrapping paper, and before she can say a word I raise my palm and bring it down hard on her bare ass.

She screams as I spank her bottom nice and hard, my oven-mitt sized palms fitting her basketball buttcheeks perfectly. I'm bleeding down my chin and half-blind with anger, but even through all of that I take care not to hurt her. I know the slaps will sting, but so long as I keep my palms on the meaty part of her ass, she'll be fine.

"Surgeon's wife needs to learn that if you start a fight by clubbing someone in the head and then kicking him in the face, there are gonna be repercussions," I bark, rubbing her reddening ass and then spanking it again until the flesh quivers in a way that makes me so hard I wish I was a worse man so I could take her right now, right here, face-down and ass-up.

But although I may be a bad man, I ain't *that* kind of bad. So I give her three more tight, well-placed smacks on her naked butt, and then I pull my hand away and sit back on my haunches, gulping hot breaths, swallowing warm blood, staring down at the most gorgeous ass either side of the Mississippi.

Her butt is red like an apple, and I reach out and gently caress her smooth, stinging skin, expecting her to recoil and maybe try to kick me in the balls. But Quinnie just turns her head to the side and whimpers as I massage her with more force, kneading her ass until I feel her move her hips.

"You all right?" I whisper, gritting my teeth and almost biting my tongue off when I realize how close I came to totally losing control. But at the same time there's a calmness in me, a solid belief that I know where the line is and I know I'm not so far gone into the darkness that I'd cross that line.

"You . . . you spanked me," she says, blinking at me and then closing her eyes and sucking in a trembling breath as I press my thumbs and fingers into her ass, slowly pulling her cheeks apart and getting a glimpse of her tight rear pucker, clean and shiny in the interior lights, a vision of dark beauty that almost makes me explode in my pants.

"You clubbed me," I say with a shrug, licking blood off my lips and blinking as the cut above my eye begins to close up. "Then you kicked me. And you almost stole my truck. Shit, you realize that if you actually did drive off with the Syndicate's load, I'd have had to call it in—which would mean you'd have a team of professional cleaners on your ass."

She opens one eye and it goes wide when she sees the damage she did to my face. But then she closes the eye and shrugs. "Still doesn't give you the right to spank me."

"If it weren't for me you'd be crocodile feed right now," I say.

"There are crocodiles in the river this far north?"

"Well, no," I say. "It was a figure of speech."

"Ah," she says. "A trucker poet. Just my luck."

I snort out a laugh. "I think it's safe to say your luck's run out."

Quinnie goes quiet. "So what now? You going to kill me like you promised?"

"Maybe."

"Go ahead. I don't care. Do it now. Go on, trucker."

I frown at her tone. There's an edge to it, like desperation being held in check. "Why'd you decide to run?" I say softly.

She shrugs against the seat, her eyes shutting again, maybe all of her shutting down. I remind myself that this woman's asshole husband just tried to kill her. Think that has an impact on a woman? Think it hurts when the man who vowed to cherish and protect you wants you tossed off a cliff? Even if she doesn't love him, that's gotta hurt inside. Hurt like hell. Make you feel like shit. Worthless. Alone. Unable to trust anyone—least of all a man.

"Never mind," I mutter, pulling at the tattered

edges of her jeans and covering her nakedness. "I understand. I'd have tried to run too. I'd have tried to fight too. You did the right thing. Maybe not the smartest thing—given that you don't know the forest and you clearly don't know how to drive a rig—but it was the right thing. I can't expect you to trust me."

Now she opens those eyes, and I see a flicker of warmth, like a candle went on somewhere in those depths. "I did trust you. That's why I ran," she says, shifting her gaze down past my blood-caked lips and then back into my half-closed eyes. "I knew you wouldn't hurt me too bad if you caught me. I knew you wouldn't kill me if you caught me. You're a criminal, but you aren't evil. Running was a good bet. If I got away, great. If I got caught, I'd just be back where we started, same as before."

I rub my head and wince. "And where were we before I got my head cracked open and my nose all bloodied?"

She giggles. "I'd asked you to kill my husband. You can name your price. After all, once he's dead, I'll be a rich widow."

I touch my lip and stretch my neck. "You don't think he already cut you out of his will?"

Quinnie nods. "I'm sure he has. But all the houses and a lot of the investments and bank accounts are held jointly, so he can't do anything about that so long as I'm alive. My name's on property and assets worth ten million plus." She winks up at me. "I'll pay you a million for his scalp."

I glance at my hunting knife and laugh. "You don't mean that," I say. "You might be pissed off enough to want him dead, but that ain't the same as having him killed." Now I reach for that knife and unsheathe it, holding the sliver blade up to the interior lights, which cast it in an eerie green glow. "Luckily you won't need to worry about having him killed. You won't need to worry about paying me a fucking dime. I'll do it for free, Quinnie. You'll have your scalp, and I'll have my revenge."

Quinnie draws a sharp breath, and then she frowns. "Revenge for what?"

I reach down and touch her cheek, my body tightening as warmth rolls through me. "Revenge for touching what's mine. Hurting what's mine. Trying to take what's mine."

She gasps like my fingers burn, and her eyes widen like moons at the equator. "I'm . . . yours?" she whispers.

I nod. "I said I might keep you. And then I decided that yeah, I'm gonna keep you." I glance down at her, tilting my head to the right and closing my throbbing left eye. "How do you feel about that?"

Quinnie purses her lips and cranes her neck so she can see her ass, and then she closes her eyes and sniffles in a way that could be laughter or sobbing or both. "I've been married twice, Quake," she says through those in-between tears. "My first husband left me for another woman. My second husband tried to kill me. They both wanted to get rid of me, Quake. You sure you want to keep me?"

"I'm sure," I say, the words coming at the speed of thought, the feeling coming at the speed of light, the certainty coming at the speed of love. I see the hurt in her brown eyes. I see what those men did to her inside. I understand it because I lived it. I had a woman do that to me. Break me open and scoop out all the good parts before tossing me aside for something fresh and new. "You're a keeper, Quinnie. And you're mine, you hear? Mine forever, and I'm gonna get you your divorce papers . . . signed in blood."

She giggles as I hold up that hunting knife, and I break a smile when I realize how ridiculous I must look with a busted nose and swollen eye and a hunting knife the size of a chainsaw.

"Signed in blood?" she says with a sweet smile and a sly gaze that reminds me that there's something in this girl, something that speaks to the darkness in me, something that brought us together, something that'll keep us together. "You really are a trucker poet."

I grin so wide my nose starts to bleed again. Then I lean close and kiss her on the cheek, her scent sending spirals of electricity down my spine, all the way to my toes. She turns her head, and I focus on those red lips that fix my double vision in an instant. I wipe my mouth to get the blood off it, but she grabs my hand and shakes her head.

And so I kiss her.

By God, I kiss her.

6
QUINNIE

He's kissing me and I'm kissing him back, my mouth opening wide for his tongue even as my mind shuts down like a bear-trap. My ass stings from that stern spanking, and I'm aroused in that desperate way that tells me I'm past the point of reason and common sense, in a state of disconnection from a reality that's too crazy to comprehend.

Am I doing this because I need Quake, I wonder as I taste his salt on my tongue, smell his musk in my nostrils, feel his heavy hips push my legs apart as I spread for him, my body slung across the massive front bench-style seat of the old-style truck. He's so big in his pants I can feel his cockhead grind against my mound. My panties are shredded, but still wrapped around my front, the soaked satin digging into my slit as Quake kisses and grinds and we gasp together between furious kisses so hot there's steam in the air.

I gave myself to Richard for money and stability, comes the thought as Quake slides his big hand around the back of my neck and kisses me harder. Am I giving myself to Quake for pretty much the same thing? Is that what I am? Is that *all* I am?

Quake pulls back just then, his face beautifully scarred, brilliantly broken, those green eyes half closed but yet focused like moonbeams. I know he's wondering the same thing: Am I doing this because I need him or because I want to?

You're a keeper, he'd whispered to me. He'd said it and I believed him—not just that he meant it, but also that it was real. That I *am* a keeper. My two husbands didn't want to keep me, but maybe that was my journey to this moment in time, this man in space, this trucker who said he wants to keep me.

Quake fists my hair and leans close, his eyes searching mine, his weight heavy on my body. "I'll stop if you say it," he whispers, letting out a shuddering breath as he drags his tongue down my cheek and along my trembling neck.

"You didn't stop yourself from spanking me like a schoolgirl," I say, blinking as a curious warmth coils down my spine. Quake's fingers are tightening in my thick hair, and he's so heavy against me it's like I'm pinned under a tractor. He could use me like that sex doll and toss me into the woods for the bears and wolves and nobody would ever know. So why the hell do I still feel safe with him? Why do I believe that he really would stop if I said it? Is this intuition? Is this the sixth sense that I ignored in the past, the instinct that whispered David wasn't the one and warned Richard wasn't the one? Is it calling to me again, begging for me to listen, forcing me into a position where I have to find the part of myself to which I refused to give voice? The part of me that at some point decided love wasn't a guarantee of anything so to hell with love and follow the money?

"I don't remember you asking me to stop spanking you," Quake says, grinning like an comic ax-murderer, his swollen eye closing up and making me wince when I remember I did that to him.

"I don't remember getting a chance to do much besides scream for my life."

Quake grunts. "And you got your life, didn't you?" He sniffs pointedly through his busted nose. "Almost got *my* life too. Shit, you can swing that club like a cavewoman."

I raise an eyebrow, shifting under his warm heft. "Cavewoman?" I think a moment and then shrug. "OK. I guess I like that better than surgeon's wife."

Quake's cheekbones tighten and his face darkens, those eyes stretching to green slits. "You aren't his wife anymore. He lost any marital privileges when he tried to murder you. Hell, he also lost the privilege to live a long and happy life. The rest of his life is going to be short and painful."

I close my eyes and shake my head, not sure why his over-the-top proclamations of what he's going to do to Richard make me tingly to my toes. Is that something I've been hiding from myself too? Am I really capable of an eye for an eye, killing the man who wanted me dead? Is Quake really capable of it?

"I'd rather see Richard rot in jail for the rest of his life," I say. "Instead of giving him an easy way out that might land *you* in jail. Or both of us, for that matter."

"You wouldn't go to jail. I ain't doing it for you. I'm doing it because I can't live knowing that piece of raccoon-shit is breathing clean air. I want him six feet under, sucking in dirt and worms with his last breath."

"You really should try some trucker poetry," I say, a sly smile breaking as I picture Richard buried alive, worms crawling into his nose, shimming up to his brain and eating him from the inside out as he screams for his frigid mother.

"Your hair is poetry," he says, sniffing my tussled locks and kissing my neck. "And your neck is . . . is . . ."

I tighten as his rough lips raise goosebumps all the way down to my nipples, and I giggle when I feel him reaching for words to complete his clumsy ode to my hair and neck. I can tell he probably just about got through high school before heading out into the world, and I sigh and touch his scarred face. Those green eyes are deep set and guarded, and my imagination drifts as I make up his past, picture the boy who was born during an earthquake, wonder if there is such a thing as destiny, if that boy was born to rumble down the open road, cracking foundations, breaking down walls, busting through brick and stone and everything in between as he tries to beat his life into a manageable shape.

We watch each other in silence, our bodies pressed together like planks of wood, limbs intertwined like roots of two old trees who've silently stood by each other for centuries. I imagine growing old with Quake, and the vision is so true I almost burst into tears. I see us somewhere in the mountains, his silver rig parked outside, our chil-

Traded to the Trucker 65

dren about to become parents themselves, even our pets now in the third generation, their bloodline coexisting with ours, mirroring the interdependence of the forest's creatures.

"Why am I seeing us old and gray together?" I whisper, touching his face again and bringing my fingers to my lips. "Happy together. Is it just wishful thinking?"

Quake blinks and looks at my fingernails speckled with his blood. "Don't know. But if that's what you're seeing, I'll take it. At least it means we come out of this alive."

I frown. "Why wouldn't we come out of this alive? Richard thinks I'm dead, and even when they don't find my body in the wreckage and he figures I made it out, what's he going to do? Clearly he doesn't have the stomach to do it himself. Man could've slit my throat any given night with his precious scalpel. And he's obsessive enough that he could've gotten rid of my body and cleaned up any evidence."

Quake moves his lower lip and cracks his jaw. He plants an elbow on either side of my head and takes some of his weight off me though I don't mind. "Maybe he's worried about what the neighbors would say. What his fellow doctors would say. What high society would say. Wife goes missing and everyone's gonna blame the husband even if he never gets convicted. But she gets killed in a car accident hundreds of miles away . . . well, then it's just an accident."

I close one eye and twist my mouth up at him. "It's almost like you know Richard," I mutter. "He's obsessed with perception, about what people think. And not just about him, but about me too."

"Like what?"

I shrug. "The way I talk. My crude jokes." I glance down at my healthy cleavage, wriggling my big hips against his. "Other stuff. Just superficial stuff."

Quake grits his teeth, and then his eyes flare. "You're shittin' me. Your body? He had the fucking nerve to . . . to . . . oh, man, he is so dead. So fucking dead."

I snicker and then smile wide as that warmth floods me again. I can't really take this macho stuff seriously—I mean, if Richard said something like that I'd laugh in his face. But somehow there's a simplicity to Quake's proclamations—an emotional simplicity that's pure like an animal's. I study those shining wolf-eyes and nod. Yes. Just like an animal doesn't burden itself with trying to lie or hide its feelings, Quake is all out there—a bit raw and unrefined, but opened up and honest. When he was angry, he spanked my ass. When he was lustful, he kissed my lips. When he decided to keep me, he looked me in the eye and said so.

"I wouldn't be surprised if that's the reason Richard wanted me gone," I say with an eye-roll. "Last year he refused to put our photograph on the Christmas card. Made some wisecrack about how he didn't want his colleagues congratulating him on my pregnancy!"

Quake licks his lips and grins tightly, digging his elbows into the seat and clenching his fists. "Oh, you are really getting me in the mood, honey. Maybe I'll slice him from the bottom up so he can watch his own guts spill out." Then he raises an eyebrow and grunts. "Though gutless snake that he is, maybe he ain't got much in there."

I wince and smile at the same time, smacking Quake lightly on the back of his head as he grins like the executioner behind the chopping block. It's a strangely light moment, almost like we're toying with the fantasy, reveling in the darkness of revenge. Will we actually do it? Probably not. I might be mad enough to kill, and nobody deserves it more than Richard. But the fantasy is playful, almost good-natured, like a child's dream of killing the bogeyman. The child knows the monster isn't real, just like I know that Richard isn't so much a monster as our marriage was monstrous. I know I never loved him, and I went into it with my eyes wide open. And Richard isn't capable of loving anyone—I knew it the first time he brought me to meet his family. I saw it in the way his parents interacted with him, with his siblings, with each other. There was no love at the dinner table, no laughter, not even much sound other than the clink of heavy silverware on bone-china plates. I'd imagined Richard being raised like a tenant in a luxury boarding house, and perhaps that sprinkle of pity had warmed me up just enough to convince myself that maybe I could show Richard how to love . . . even if I didn't love him.

And now suddenly I feel sorry for Richard, and my throat almost closes up as I wonder if I'm in denial, convincing myself that Richard can be forgiven, that maybe I'm partly responsible. It almost sickens me, and I bite my lip and stare up at the fake-leather ceiling of the truck, hating my thoughts for revealing my weakness, hating myself for even *considering*that maybe I don't hate Richard.

But then I feel Quake stroke my hair, and I focus on his eyes and feel the smile come back, feel thoughts of Richard slither away like a snake in the sun. And suddenly I understand why I can't hate Richard.

It's because you can't hate when you're in love.

"Quake, listen," I whisper, kissing his hand as he runs his fingers along my cheek. "I spent half my life saying the words without ever meaning them. Now I'm scared to say those same words because they mean so much. I'm scared of what I feel, Quake. Scared that it's the situation, that it's the desperation, that it's the part of me that knows sex is a weapon, that it can be used to manipulate and enslave, to deceive and even to destroy."

Quake takes a slow, heavy breath, squaring his jaw as his eyes roam my face. "Then we won't have sex," he says in that simple way that carries a complexity that would take years to comprehend. "You've been scared enough today, Quinnie. Shit, your whole world just got shattered, babe. No shit you're turned around. Messed up. Not sure which way is up. Not sure whom to trust. Not even sure if you can trust yourself, probably." He gently pulls himself off me, reaching to a shelf above the back bench and grabbing a folded set of green cargo-pants that still have the label on the loop. "You're safe with me, Quinnie. I don't care how long it takes for you to believe that, but you're safe with me."

I take the clothes and hold them against my chest as I watch this trucker-criminal who just spanked me raw act more gentlemanly than any man in my past. It should be incongruous, but all I get from him is the unshakable honesty of a tree. He means what he says, and I'm slowly coming around to letting myself believe anything he says.

And that permission to believe breaks through all the way when he turns to me and speaks his next truth:

"You might be scared, Quinnie. You might be unsure, uneasy, undecided. But I ain't any of those things. I meant what I said, and my word means something since I got nothing else of value. I'm keeping you, Quinnie. You're a keeper, and I'm keeping you, no matter how many ex-husbands I need to bury along the way."

7
<u>QUAKE</u>

"How many bodies you buried today?" I nod at the shovel the Syndicate guy is dragging in his left hand as he circles around to check the seal on the load I just unhitched in the carefully camouflaged loading-bay a few miles before the Canadian border crossing.

"You don't wanna know," he grunts, wiping his brow and shooting me a look that tells me my joke wasn't a joke after all. He shines his flashlight on the electronic lock and grunts. "Looks good. Your envelope is in the usual spot in the shack."

I nod, glancing back at my rig to make sure Quinnie can't be seen from down here. She's laying down in the back bench and no one ever checks my cab, but I'm still on edge. Usually I'm loose and relaxed at the end of a run—after all, I'm home free, with cash in my pocket and the open road ahead of me. But Quinnie's changed everything for me, and although I told her straight-faced that I wasn't scared, truth is I'm fucking terrified of what I feel, of how fierce that protective fire blazes, how deep that need to burn away her past runs.

I'm all inside my head as I hurry to the shack and grab my cash from the numbered lockbox. I don't bother to count it. The Syndicate's never shorted me a dollar in ten years. They're as professional as it gets. Everything they do is surgically precise.

"Though maybe surgeons aren't that precise," I mutter as I mull over the oddness of that guy Richard hiring a couple of goons to run Quinnie off the road. That's a pretty risky operation, ain't it? Too many things could go wrong. Doesn't fit that an obsessive surgeon would come up with a such a loose plan. How did he even get in touch with those guys? Syndicate guys don't do outside jobs. Maybe the Black Car dudes were contractors like me, doing jobs now and then but not on the regular payroll. Syndicate doesn't do that anymore, though. I'm grandfathered in on account of my history of delivering the goods.

I'm almost back at the truck when the rising sun reflects off a parked car and sends splinters of light into my darned eyes. I grimace and turn, doing a double-take when I see it's a busted-up black car that looks familiar.

"No way," I mutter, my spine stiffening as I think back to that shovel. I freeze, rubbing my jaw and looking both ways as my mind spins so fast it hurts behind my eyes. I glance back at the shack, wondering if those guys came here to get fixed up. But there's nobody inside, and so I hurry back to my truck and climb in, confusion and dread rising in me like a twin-headed snake.

Soon we're down the road and well out of sight, and I give Quinnie the all clear, smiling as she pops up like a jack-in-the-box and squeezes her beautifully curvy body between the seats, almost kicking me again before she manages to buckle in as my shotgun rider. I think about that black car and the shovel. Then I smile at her and take her hand, my other hand on the wheel, my eyes on the road.

"You think they've found my car yet?" she says.

I glance at the dashboard clock. Almost seven. "Sun's been up for almost an hour. Someone probably saw the broken guardrail with all the glass and plastic scattered around. So yeah. Figure Richard will get the call within the hour if he hasn't already."

I look down at her, only now remembering she's wearing my spare cargo-pants which are nice and snug on those wide hips. "You lost your phone in the crash, right?"

She nods. "Or those thugs took it when I was passed out. Wallet and cash is gone too, so yeah. It must have been those guys."

I swallow hard and tighten my grip on the wheel. "So your phone might be with those guys? In their car?"

She looks at me and shrugs. Then her eyes go wide and she mouths an expletive and slams back into the seat. "Shit. If Richard was able to track my car, maybe he's also tracking my phone! Which would mean he'd see that my phone and my car weren't in the same place! Which would mean—"

"He knows you're alive," I grunt, reaching for the GPS, punching in C-H-I and selecting Chicago. "He must have known all night." Again my mind snaps back to that black car in the Syndicate's truck bay, and I feel a connection gnawing at me even though it might just be coincidence. Maybe those guys switched cars at the truck bay. Maybe that shovel was for burying treasure and not those guys' executed bodies.

Or maybe I underestimated this guy Richard.

Maybe we both did.

One look at Quinnie and I see the wheels turning, feel the fear rising, sense the dread digging in. If Richard could get those two guys killed by the Syndicate, it means he's connected to the Syndicate. It's sure as hell possible—after all, the Syndicate is like a big corporation, and like any corporation it has shareholders. And contrary to what you see on TV, crime does in fact pay. It pays big, and I've heard rumors of underground stock exchanges where criminal enterprises like the Syndicate get funding for their mischief. I guess the nerdy millionaire investors get a thrill out of feeling like gangsters even though they wouldn't know how to bust their way out of a sandwich bag.

"Quinnie, listen," I say after weighing whether to keep it to myself. "I saw that black car parked in the truck bay. It was empty. Can't say for certain, but my gut tells me those guys were taken out by the Syndicate. Loose ends being tied up." I swallow hard as I feel her gasp and then close her eyes tight. I take her hand and she hangs on tight like a kid. "And I sure as hell don't know anything else for sure, but my gut's telling me Richard is more than he seems."

Quinnie's face is peaked, her eyes wide, her skin pale with streaks of red. But she keeps her jaw tight and nods before looking over at me. "What do you think those guys said before they were taken out? Said about me? And you?"

I blink and close my eyes tight, groaning when I realize she's right. Those fuckers would have talked—and even if they didn't, those other Syndicate guys at Trucker's Paradise could've said something.

"We have to assume Richard knows about my truck, about me, that you're with me," I say. Then I frown and glance over at her. "But that's a good thing," I add, grinning at her puzzlement. "He thinks I traded for you so I can use you and then lose you," I say with a shrug. "He doesn't know I'm keeping you. That you're mine." I drop my left arm down and touch my hunting knife. "And that we're coming for him."

"We're what?" she says before noticing the GPS re-routing us to Highway 94 East, which will blow us right into the Windy City. "Quake, what are you doing?"

I don't even look at her. "What's gotta be done. If Richard is connected to the Syndicate, we can't run and we can't hide. We'll be running forever, hiding forever, and that's not my thing. Too complicated for my simple mind. I'm old-school, Quinnie. I'm going to walk in the front door, tell Richard his woman now belongs to me, and then end it like a man."

Quinnie glances at me and then focuses on the road again. But I saw something in those eyes, felt something in that look, sensed something in her breath. She's scared, but she's also excited. She thinks I'm over-the-top insane, but she also understands that running and hiding isn't a long term fix. She's in this with me, and I suddenly decide I can trust her. Yeah, she clocked me good back there, tried to escape with my truck. But that was the last gasp of the woman she used to be. Now she's my woman, and my woman understands that I tell it like it is, I see it like it is, I take it like it is.

"All right," she says softly, dropping her arm down between us so I can hold her hand again. "All right, Quake. I'm in it for the long haul. In it with you."

And I grin wide and honk the bullhorn, opening up the throttle and chugging my rig down the oil-black road, rolling towards the fire, roaring to the finale, rumbling to our forever.

8
NINETEEN HOURS LATER
CHICAGO
QUINNIE

"We've been driving forever," I groan, stretching my arms out wide and poking Quake in the ear. "I didn't realize this country was so big."

"City slicker," he teases as we roll down the Dan Ryan Expressway, the gray spires of Chicago looming at the end of the winding black road like the cursed City of Sodom. "Where am I going, Quinnie? Which exit?"

I pull at my lower lip as the anxiety coiled up inside springs out when I realize this shit is real, that I'm within a few miles of that snake Richard, within a few hours of crossing the point of no return. "Depends," I say slowly. "There's the downtown penthouse, but we've also got an estate in Lake Forest, up near Lake Michigan, just outside the city. Where would you be today, Richard?"

Now I think back to Richard's obsessiveness when it comes to what "people" say, and immediately I know he wouldn't want to be at work or in a highrise condo building with doormen and mailmen and neighbors all asking about his missing-and-presumed-dead wife. So I take over the GPS and put in our Lake Forest address as Quake grunts and changes gears, his left hand dropping down again, those rough fingers caressing the leather-bound hilt of his hunting knife.

I shake my head and instinctively reach for my phone—which of course isn't there. "Can I use your phone to check the news?" I ask. Quake just frowns like he doesn't understand, and when I see the two old-style flip-phones in the tray beneath the dash, I sigh and roll my eyes. "Radio it is," I mutter, poking the big plastic buttons until I find the local news.

We sit through updates about the Bulls, the Cubs,

the Sox, and even the Major League Soccer team, and finally my ears tingle at the mention of a local man's missing wife.

"Wait, that's not me," I say, turning up the volume and staring at Quake, who's frowning so deep his cuts are starting to bleed again.

A Chicago woman reported missing last night has been found dead. Her body was recovered from Lake Michigan. Initial police reports are that she took her boat out alone and fell overboard. There was no suicide note, no sign of foul play, and police insiders expect the Medical Examiner to rule the death an accident. The woman is survived by her husband, local businessman David Duff.

The name sets off so many bells in my head I almost slap myself to make it stop. Quake's saying something, but even when the bells stop I can't hear shit. All I get is that deafening whine you get when the TV station is off the air. Somehow I manage to turn off the radio and take a couple of breaths so I don't pass out. Then I run my fingers through my hair, pulling at a knot so hard I wince. The pain brings me back to my senses, and I bite my lip and swallow hard before turning to Quake.

"It can't be," I whisper. "Maybe there's a different David Duff in Chicago. That's probably a common name, right?"

Quake shoots me a concerned look and then shrugs. "Who the hell is David Duff?"

I rub my burning eyes and shake my throbbing head. "David is my . . ." I mumble as that whine comes back until my head sounds like a beehive in spring. "He's my first husband. David's my first husband."

Quake's eyes go wide like tennis balls, and he whips his head back and forth between me and the road. He changes lanes so fast we get a long, angry honk from a red minivan, and both of us raise our middle fingers at the same time. It would be funny if not for the sickening dread curling through our insides, the feeling that something's going on and you don't know what it is but it's not good. It is *not* good.

Quake finally breaks the deafening silence. "Sicilian wife swap," he says. "Fuck, they're pulling the Sicilian wife swap!"

I glance at him, somehow managing to widen my eyes and frown at the same time, which probably isn't good for my worry-lines. "Great," I say, smiling frantically like a lunatic on a moonless night. "The Sicilian Wife Swap. Of course!"

Quake raises an eyebrow. Then he exhales hard and keeps his eyes straight ahead. "You kill my wife, I kill yours," he says softly. "Complicates things for any investigator—especially if both murders look like accidents." He shrugs and grunts. "Looks like Richard took care of David's wife pretty clean. Boating accident is solid—no witnesses, no cameras, and even a good swimmer is eventually gonna drown if they're dropped in the middle of Lake Michigan."

I rub the back of my neck and feel something crack. I twist my back and get another crack, and suddenly I'm feeling alert like I got plugged into the wall outlet. "So *David* was the one who tried to kill me?"

Quake steals a sideways glance at me and then rubs his jaw. "Hate to break it to you, honey, but they *both* tried to kill you."

I rub my forehead and blink away some stars. "Ohmygod, *both* my husbands tried to kill me."

"Don't take it personal," he says.

I almost scratch his green eyes out. "Easy for you to say," I snarl. "Kinda hard not to wonder why every man in my life wants me dead."

Quake shrugs those big shoulders like he's almost amused. Or maybe excited that he gets to wipe out both my ex-husbands. I guess that's what a caveman would do in the old days. Hell, a caveman would probably eat the other man's kids too.

Thank heavens I didn't get knocked up by either of those monsters!

But now I wonder if I'm the monster in all this. What does this say about me? Am I clueless about how horrible I am?

"What's wrong with me?" I mutter, moving my head in little side-to-side spurts like a malfunctioning bobblehead doll. "How long before you use that knife on me, Quake?"

Quake snaps his head toward me, his eyebrows deep in a V, green eyes fierce and honest. He clenches his jaw so hard his lips go white, and then he reaches for that big knife and places it on my lap. "Go on. Slide it out."

I force a chuckle, but Quake doesn't flinch.

"Do what I say," he says, his voice low, deep, commanding.

I swallow hard. Then I grasp the thick bison-leather handle and slide the knife out of its brown deerskin sheath. The blade is broad and clean with a quicksilver shine so true I can see my face in the bright steel. I hold it up and let out a trembling breath as a ripple of energy goes up my spine.

"Feels good, don't it?"

I just nod as that ripple of power gets to my throat, taking my voice and my breath at the same time. "What is this feeling?" I mutter, touching my forehead to see if I have a fever. I don't. If anything I'm cold. Cold like steel. Cold like revenge.

"I ain't much good at naming feelings," Quake says.

I nod. "I'm usually pretty good at naming feelings. But this one doesn't have a name. It feels too deep, too raw, too . . . too ancient."

We glide off the highway as I hold that knife tight, let that primordial power ooze through me like dark magic. I don't know what's happening to me, but I don't want it to stop. I close my eyes and breathe slow and deep like I'm meditating, and my lips tremble as I wonder if I'm to blame for this, if my choices to marry those men means I'm somehow responsible.

"You ain't responsible for their choices," Quake whispers through my trance, his voice drifting over the engine's low growl. "Don't you dare complicate this with your thinking, you hear? Listen to that still, silent part of you, the part that's ancient, just like you said. I feel that part of me when I'm alone on the road, when my thoughts shut down and there's nothing but feeling. Feelings that don't got names. Ancient feelings, just like you said."

I nod dumbly, taking a last look at the blade before sheathing it as we get within a few miles of my Lake Forest home. Richard never liked this place, but I loved it. It's got some good acreage, lake access, and old trees that have been here longer than people have.

"Still and silent," I whisper as I see the treetops in the distance. "What is that stillness? What is that silence?" I glance at Quake as he rolls to a smooth stop a couple of miles from the gates. He shrugs like he doesn't need to name that stillness, that he's comfortable with namelessness, with feeling without words, sensation without speech.

And as I study Quake in profile, I get the sudden feeling of the most profound connection with him, a devastating realization that at the bottom of that grunty simplicity lies the wisdom of that stillness, the intelligence of that silence, the power of the primal. And now I sense that ancient part of me reaching out to that stillness in him, and it's like I *know* we're connected, that this whole journey was about us, that we're in love at the most simple level, like two single-celled creatures crawling towards each other, pulled together by that same mysterious life force . . .

The force called love.

"I love you, Quake," I whisper as he kills the engine and plunges us into stillness that shakes me to the core. "I've said those words to men I never loved, and only now do I understand what it feels like to mean those words. I love you, Quake. And I'm ready for anything, so long as you're with me."

Quake's breath catches, and his swollen eye throbs as my words sink in. He exhales slowly, reaches out and cups my face, draws me in for a tender kiss that burns like starfire. I blink and touch his rough, scarred face, and I see that stillness in his green eyes like I'm suddenly tuned in to that ancient consciousness. Is that what the soul is? The eternal, unbreakable, unshakeable part of us? Is that what happens when you fall in love? You get to see through the complexity until things are so fucking simple it scares you, shakes you, shatters you . . .

"I love you too, Quinnie," come the simple words from my trucker-poet-criminal-killer, and I smile when he smoothes my knotted hair flat and slides that oversized hand to the back of my neck.

I shiver as he tightens his grip and pulls me in for another kiss. This one isn't gentle like the first, and I gasp when I see how hard Quake is, how his pants are peaked like the Sears Tower, his green eyes narrowed with lust. I'm heating up too, and I remember how Quake backed off earlier when he sensed I was uncomfortable, not ready to take that step with a stranger.

"You don't feel like a stranger, Quake," I whisper, biting his lip and then letting him take my mouth in his for a savage kiss. "Those other men feel like strangers. Even the woman I was just yesterday feels like a stranger. But you . . . you feel like . . . like forever, Quake. Yes. That's it. You feel like forever."

Quake grins and drags his rough thumb against my smooth cheek. "We naming things again?"

I shrug, and then I gasp when he slams his lips into mine, drives his tongue into my mouth, and takes my breasts firmly in this hands all in one breathtakingly swift move that makes me so wet so fast I almost come in my panties.

But then I remember I'm not wearing panties, that this beast ripped them to ribbons when he smacked my bottom like frontiersmen used to do to get their mail-order brides to obey. It's a weird thought. It's also the last thought, because now Quake's snapped my buttons off and has popped my bra up over my boobs and is pinching my nipples so hard they're dark red and pointy like porcupines. He sucks each until I'm groaning and panting, and when I feel his hand slide between my legs, fingers jamming the rough cloth of my loaner pants into my wet bush, I arch my neck back so fast I bump my head against the closed window.

"In the back," he says, the words barked like an order. "Now."

I don't hesitate, immediately squeezing my hips between the seats and landing on my ass in the back bench. With a squeal I move aside so I don't get crushed by Quake's mass as he launches himself through the seats, making them both snap back furiously as they creak in protest.

My loaner plaid shirt is gone and I don't know where. My pants are off and I don't know how. Suddenly I'm naked on fake leather, my pussy so wet I'm leaving warm streaks all over the seat. Quake leans down and sniffs my crotch, and then he's on me like a beast, licking my face like an animal marking his mate, biting my neck like a wolf at play, sucking my breasts like he wants to drink me up, fingering my cunt like he's searching for secrets.

He finds my secret a moment later, curling a middle finger thicker than a bratwurst up my vagina and tapping the upper wall like he knows where my fibrous spot lies hidden.

"Oh, *shit*!" I scream, my eyes snapping wide and then rolling up in my head as I come suddenly and violently, squirting all over his hand and then his

Traded to the Trucker 89

face when he gets down there and starts to lap at my pussy like a lion at a mountain spring.

I come again, all over Quake's face, my boobs convulsing as my climax rocks me. Quake slides his tongue into my hole and jabs back and forth, his hands grasping my buttcheeks and spreading them as he tongue-fucks me to a crushing crescendo that has me clawing at the metal walls.

I come hard and long, and just when I feel things leveling off, Quake's fingers claw their way to my asscrack, his thumb tapping my rear pucker and then pressing down like a plug. The sensation is so unexpectedly filthy that I dig my nails deep into his shoulder and buck my hips into his face. His thumb plunges into my asshole, and I come again, this time so hard I'm drooling all over my chin like a baby.

"Oh, fuck, babe," he pants, raising his head from between my legs, licking his lips and swallowing. He leans in and kisses me on the lips so I can taste my own pussy, and then he grins and goes back on his knees, his massive body taking up so much space it's like we're locked in a coffin together, with nothing to do but fuck each other to death.

Quake rips off his tank top and unbuckles his rawhide belt, sliding it past the loops so fast I smell the burn. His bulge is obscene, and when he unbuttons and unzips his cock springs out with such fury I get sprayed all the way to my neck with his sticky pre-cum.

His size startles me, and I claw at the slick seat, panting as he drags his bulbous, shining cockhead along my slit, against my clit, around my belly button, circling each nipple and then marking my neck, chin, and lips with his oil before straddling my chest and petting my hair while I swallow hard and stare up at his traincar-thick shaft that's dripping all over me.

I take him into my mouth without a word, and he groans and pushes himself down my throat as I hurriedly open for him. There's no hesitation in this man, but at the same time I sense that he's in control of himself, that he's supremely aware of my body and what it can take, how much it can take. It's very much an extension of Quake's simplicity, his unquestioning trust in his own instinct, his own silence, his own stillness.

I stare up into his face as I suck him, and I almost smile when I see his eyes clamped shut, a huge smile on his scarred face, his rough lips shining with my pussy-juice as his tongue whips about like he can't help himself.

His balls are large and heavy like sandbags swinging against my throat, and when I gently cup them as he fucks me in the mouth, Quake groans and curses and then pulls out before he comes.

His cock bounces as he slides down along my body, and I'm all wet from my saliva and his pre-cum and everything in between. I take deep gulps of air, the clean musk of his cock still filling my nostrils and making me so ready to be fucked it scares me. For some reason I think about how it felt to hold that knife, and when Quake presses his cockhead against my opening and then plunges all the way into my cunt, I groan as that ancient feeling of stillness roars through me like an explosion in space, where there's no sound but just feeling, feeling so overwhelming that it can't be named, can't be controlled, can't be stopped.

And then Quake is all the way inside me, his thickness spreading my inner walls so wide my mouth opens in sympathy. He flexes inside and holds himself there, groaning and then looking down at me with eyes that carry just one emotion

. . .

An emotion that has a name.
Its name is love.
Pure and simple.
Love.

9
QUAKE

Love. That's the only name for it. Even though I ain't into naming things, I sure as hell know this thing's name. No question about it. This is love, and I know because I've never felt this before. Not with that ex-wife. Not with any woman who ever rode shotgun with me. Hell, not even in my drunken days back when I used to rage with the bikers and their babes. Yeah, this is love. And who woulda thought I'd find it with a surgeon's wife.

But she ain't just some doctor's wife slumming it with a trucker, I think as I kiss her lips and move inside her, making her moan out her mouth and drip out her cunt. She found that stillness in her. I saw her find it when she looked at herself in that clean steel, that knife's edge, that reminder that violence runs in our blood as strong as sex. The need to kill is as ancient as the need to fuck. Every beast that hunts knows this. Humans know it too, but we're forced to bury it in the darkness of our souls, hide it away and pretend like it ain't there.

But it's there.

It's always there.

Hiding in the stillness.

Crouching in the silence.

Buried so deep that when it escapes it twists and turns like a tree-root seeking the source. That's why Richard and David were able to do what they did. It's that old blood-lust that's built into our souls coming out in them in ugly ways because they were never able to channel that energy right. Shit, I bet they don't even know the reasons they came up with their murder pact. It's that indirect thrill, just like those investors who put money into the Syndicate and feel like bad-ass gangsters while eating finger-foods at some poolside party.

But this high-class woman got a glimpse of what lies in every human heart, and I gotta make sure it gets channeled right, I think as I pull back and ram my way home again, my pelvis slamming between her hips as she screams and wraps those thick legs around my muscular ass.

And that means she's gonna be holding that knife when it's all said and done, I decide as I wrap her hair around my fingers and pull, my next thrust going so deep her eyes pop big and then go white as she wails.

Now I'm getting close, and she's so wet my balls are sticky from her pussy dripping all over me as I slam against her. We're going faster and faster, like we're in a fever dream, the adrenaline of these past two days mixing with the euphoria of finding each other, the combination churning and frothing like witch's brew, eye of newt and the glint of steel in every violent thrust, every twisted shout, every heated kiss.

My wounds are bleeding again, and the pain and arousal have me by the throat. Still I go faster, gritting my teeth as I feel Quinnie's legs tighten around me just enough to let me know she's OK, she's with me, she's built to handle me, to handle this, to handle *us*.

Her nails are ripping my back to shreds, and I smell my blood in the air as my balls begin to send my thick semen up my shaft for the biggest delivery of my trucking life. We're both shouting as my climax thunders home, but when it hits there's nothing but silence, nothing but stillness, nothing but that feeling that the universe has seen this before, played this game before, loves the game so much that it's the *only* game it plays.

The game of love.

And now sound explodes into existence, and I roar as I explode into Quinnie, my shaft tightening, my balls clenching, my cock shooting what feels like torrents of semen like a river raging downhill.

Quinnie wails as I come inside her. Her eyes are clamped shut, her pretty face twisted in a grimace of ecstasy, her lips convulsing with pleasure, her heels digging into me as I pump her full until she's overflowing down her asscrack and onto the seat.

She's coming too, and I feel her pussy clench and release like she's milking me. Somehow she coaxes more out of me, and with a groan I come again with the last of me.

And then I collapse on Quinnie, spent but whole, broken but complete, silent but with a single word spinning through the steam of my closed truck.

One word.

The only word.

Love.

10
QUINNIE

"I love these purple wildflowers," I whisper as we step lightly on the carpet of pine-needles that cover the outer reaches of our estate. "This is the first year they've been back in like a decade. Hopefully that's a good sign."

Quake glances at the vibrant purple blooms that grow on the low branches of some of the trees. "Yeah, it's a great sign," he says with a grin. "Those flowering vines sink their thirsty roots into the tree-bark. If they keep coming back every year, they can kill a tree by slowly sucking out all the sugar and nutrients."

I turn halfway and raise an eyebrow. Then I shrug. "Sounds like my marriages. Though I'm not sure if I'm the tree or the flower. Maybe a little of both."

Quake playfully nudges me as we move through the woods like kids in an enchanted forest. But then the house comes into view, and we both stop as the mood suddenly changes. Quake steps in front of me, holding a small scope to his eyes. I glance at the hunting knife hanging from his belt, and I get a strange urge to hold its warm handle, to look at its cold blade.

Quake had asked me to stay in the truck and to call the police at the first sign of trouble, but I'd ended the conversation without even bothering to argue. I already knew Quake was going to take me with him.

And I already knew I was going to go with him.

"Is that Richard?" he says, handing me the scope. I glance through it and nod. "He's alone. What about other folks? Security guys? Gardeners? Maids? Butlers?"

"Butlers?" I say, my eyebrows twitching, neck hairs bristling. "Who has *butlers* these days! Anyway, no. None of that. Richard hates having random people around. He pays for all that stuff to be done when we're out of the house."

Quake slides the scope into his side pocket and looks around. "What about weapons? Guns?"

I chuckle and shake my head. "Richard? Guns? Yeah, right. He's scared of guns."

"Everyone should be scared of guns," Quake says.

"I don't use them myself. Besides, they're noisy and they leave all kinds of evidence. Good. Come on. Let's go around front."

"Front door?"

"Sure. Why, you want me to toss you through the window?" Quake says with a grin. He grabs my hand and leads me around to the front. "Come on. Let's see what he has to say."

"Um, OK," I say, stumbling as Quake pulls me along. He pauses to make sure I'm OK, and when I nod we break from the tree cover and stride up to the front door. I'm uneasy, but Quake's right. This isn't an action movie where we shatter the windows and kill everyone inside. This is a drama where I get to confront my murderous husband before my trucker boyfriend and I slit his throat.

Quake reaches for the knocker, but suddenly the screech of tires makes us jump. Quake pulls me off the stoop and into a thicket of bougainvillea that are thankfully in bloom. We crouch down, Quake shielding me with his body, his right hand on the hilt of his knife.

I don't recognize the car, but I recognize the driver. "It's David," I whisper. Quake nods like he isn't surprised. I'm not surprised either. No doubt Richard called David so they could figure out what went wrong and whether I was dead or not—whether the trucker had tossed my used-up body in the river or not.

Richard yanks open the door before David knocks, and my straight-laced surgeon husband is so steamed-up I almost want to poke my head out and stick my tongue at him.

"You're a fucking *idiot!*" Richard says.

"And you're a fucking *liar!*" David snaps. "You didn't tell me you were married to Quinnie! That's my ex-wife! You set me up so if things went wrong, the trail would lead to me!"

"Well, things *have* gone wrong," Richard says, stepping out onto the landing and closing the door behind him. "But don't worry about the trail leading back to you."

"Why not?"

"Because they aren't going to find you, David. Man, you *are* a fucking idiot. Quinnie really knows how to pick them."

"Aren't going to find me? What the fuck does that—"

David's words drown in a gurgle that chills me to my toes, and I cover my mouth so I don't scream at the sight of David stumbling backwards, his hands holding his own throat, dark blood pouring through his fingers. He twists and turns on the stoop like a marionette doing a dance, and finally his eyes roll up in his head, his grip weakens, and he collapses in a heap, blood spurting out from his surgically sliced carotid artery.

A moment later Richard's dragging David's still-warm body off the stoop and onto the dirt on the other side of the path. He glances around, wipes his mouth with his sleeve, and then reaches into his back pocket for a set of blue medical gloves.

I'm hyperventilating into my hand, but Quake calms me with a heavy hand on my trembling shoulder. He wants me to wait, and I nod without taking my hand away from my mouth.

Soon it becomes clear to me why Quake wanted me to wait. Richard always planned to kill David to clean up that loose end, and I watch as my husband grunts and heaves David's body into a wheelbarrow and pushes it towards the thickest part of the woods on the east side of the house.

"Probably got a grave already dug," Quake says. "Must have decided to kill David all along. Nice way to seal it airtight. You getting away is a twist, but he's probably thought about it. Still, we have an edge—he doesn't know for sure that you got away. He's still hoping I kept my word, my end of the trade."

"Kept your promise, you mean," I say, glancing up at him, my heart finally slowing down as the shock works its way out. "Which you didn't, by the way."

Quake shrugs. "Didn't keep the promise. Decided to keep you instead."

I laugh, shaking my head and blinking as that vivid image of David bleeding out plays on repeat but in a shockingly peaceful way, like there's something in me that can handle the blood, witness the violence, stay strong in the face of the sinister.

"Come on," I say, glancing towards where Richard disappeared and then fighting my way out of the bougainvillea. "Let's wait for him inside. This is my house, after all."

11
QUAKE

"This is my house, after all," Quinnie says. "Why shouldn't I be here? Oh, right. Because I should be dead! Is that it, Richard? Say it. Come on. I want to hear it from you, dear husband."

I press my back against the kitchen wall, my knife unsheathed and ready, my body coiled like a spring. I can be at Richard's throat in a flash, but I'm edgy as hell after seeing what the sinister surgeon can do with his weapon of choice. Still, Quinnie insisted on talking to him, and that woman's got some steel in her spine when it comes to an argument.

Richard doesn't answer her leading question, and I know he's spinning through every paranoid scenario. Quinnie told me about that phone call just before she got run off the road. Richard said the call was a farewell. Common sense tells me this is insane, that of course Richard's going to go for her throat. But my gut tells me different, and so does Quinnie, so I gotta go with that.

"Yes," says Richard finally. "You should be dead. Why aren't you?"

I peek out and see Quinnie sit herself down on a loveseat covered in white linen. I smile and shake my head. Attagirl. No way Richard tries to cut her while she's sitting there. The blood would get all over. Deep into the cushion. Not to mention between the floorboards. Nope. He's not gonna try it in here. He's going to try to get her out of the house, onto the dirt.

"Because you asked David to do your dirty work," she says sweetly. "David wasn't much of a details guy. How'd you two meet, anyway? Underground sex club? You two had masks on and were giving each other hand-jobs when the topic of those pesky wives popped up?"

Richard grins so tight I hear his teeth spark. "There's that obscene humor that you think is so fucking cute but is pure filth. You never belonged in high society, Quinnie. Always talking like trailer trash at black-tie events. Always rolling your eyes when I say your behavior reflects on me. Your looks reflect on me. *You* reflect on me."

Quinnie's eyes go wide and she snorts and then shakes her head. "So *that's* what this is about? I . . . I *embarrass* you? That's it? Hah! You say my jokes are crude and filthy? Well, you're the joke here, Richard. A sad, pitiful joke."

Richard shrugs, rubbing the back of his spindly neck. I narrow my eyes and think back to how Richard probably doesn't understand his motivation, doesn't understand that he's so far removed from his primal masculinity, his natural humanity, that he's blaming her for this unnamable anxiety that's ripping him apart, this inexplicable angst that bubbles up in him like filthy water at the bottom of a well. Does she know what she's doing? Does she know that she's going to push him over the edge by pushing those buttons? Does she know that when nameless emotions go to the darkness in a man the results can be—

And then suddenly Richard whips out his scalpel, and with a roar I leap like a tiger, knife raised, eyes focused, every ounce of man in me concentrated on protecting my woman.

But before I can get there I see a flash of red, and I howl as I knock Richard over and raise my blade, my eyes wild at the thought that he got to my woman!

Then I see the scalpel drop from Richard's limp arm.

And I see the thin, surgically precise mark on his neck, the fresh blood so thick it looks black as oiled sin.

"What . . ." I mutter, whipping my head back and forth between Quinnie and Richard before it hits me that the doctor sliced his own fucking throat! "Why?" I say, even as the answer hits me though the words still escape my grasp.

Quinnie sighs and shakes her head slowly. "I can't explain exactly why, but I felt it in him. All those years of living that buttoned-down existence, repressing things that needed to be channeled, not blocked. Yeah, he killed David. But that was a cold kill. Planned and scheduled, just like removing a pesky appendix. Somehow I sensed he wouldn't be able to do a hot-blooded kill, that when he snapped he would fold inwards, like a building collapsing on itself."

She sighs again as I sink into the loveseat beside her. I'm still holding the clean blade, and she places her hand over mine as we stare in peaceful silence, sit in calm stillness, share a moment that feels like something without a name . . .

Something old.

Something ancient.

Something that's a part of our history on this planet.

And something that's part of our story.

Part of our forever.

12
THE NEXT DAY
QUINNIE

I watch from the window as Quake drives his rig down the cobblestones and parks it out front. The police and medical examiners left an hour ago. Quake and I didn't touch Richard's body, and so the investigators were able to reconstruct the scene and conclude the wound was self-inflicted. The police ran the plates on David's car and searched the property, finding the fresh grave that somehow had one of those purple wildflowers already digging its suckers into the soil.

"Any trouble with the cops?" Quake asks, his scent entering the house before his shadow.

I shake my head, my attention drifting like the breeze in those woods. "No. Told them I wasn't sure what happened with my accident, that I was thrown clear and hitched my way home. When I got here there was a strange car in the driveway, and Richard was dead on the floor."

"Good," says Quake, sliding his arm around my waist. "They can put together the rest. Or not, since it don't matter much now. Can't put two dead guys in jail. Hell, we could've just buried them both out here and saved everyone the trouble. I bet the cops are thinking that too. I bet that's the last we hear from them, Quinnie. They'll have no more questions."

I nod and lean my head against his hard chest. I'm not asking any more questions either, I think as I look out the window at the carefully designed rock garden that's popping with those purple wildflowers that I'm seeing everywhere now.

Wildflowers that are maybe a sign after all. A signpost to remind us that along with beauty comes brutality, that just because humans wear clothes and get their hair done it doesn't mean we aren't part of the ebb and flow of life. We aren't immune to the violence of the woods. We aren't protected from the fierceness of the forest.

Quake kisses my hair and squeezes my side as we glance into the dark woods, and I imagine my past buried out there just like it'll always be buried inside me, fertile soil from which the wildflowers of my forever blooms. The thought brings me a strange peace tinged with both sadness and joy, melancholy and excitement, darkness and light, and in my mind those old trees will always be the tombstones of my redemption, marking metaphorical graves that will soon be overrun by the green forest, the brown earth reclaiming what was always its own, the blue universe sighing as it completes another cycle in its neverending journey, another verse in its eternal poem, another chapter in its ongoing story.

The story of duality.

The story of opposites.

The story of good and bad, laughter and tears, death and rebirth.

The story of me and him.

Here and now.

Always and forever.

∞

EPILOGUE
TEN YEARS LATER
QUAKE

"It's called a double clutch. Your legs are still too short to reach the pedals." I grin at nine-year old Quaneira as she pouts at me from the passenger seat of my trusty old rig that's pretty much a museum piece now that most trucks have gone electric.

Doesn't matter, since I don't drive the long haul anymore, I think as Quest, Quaneira's twin brother, squeezes into the cab. Outside I can hear Quinnie speaking sternly to our five-year old triplets, who've been nibbling on those purple wildflowers and then showing everyone their indigo-streaked tongues.

Traded to the Trucker 111

"Let them learn the hard way," I call to my wife (who's pregnant again, by the way—my money's on quadruplets this time. I came so hard in her the night before her birthday that I just *know* four of my guys crossed the border into the holy land. Of course, just to make extra-sure I've been banging my babe nightly even though she's popping like a pumpkin. I don't remember my high school science, but I think I can get her even*more* pregnant if I fuck her hard enough . . . ;))

"These wildflowers are poisonous," Quinnie yells at me even though the truck windows are down and the warm summer breeze is lazy like a well-fed python.

I nudge our older kids and chuckle. "You guys used to eat those flowers all the time when you were kids, right?"

"They made me hallucinate," says Quaneira.

"They made me throw up," says Quest. "And hallucinate."

"OK, I do *not* need you guys freaking me out right now!" Quinnie shouts, smiling as she waddles her pregnant butt over to the truck and glares up at the three of us. I shoot a glance down her blue cotton top, shifting on my seat when I see that her boobs are plumping out with that sweet cream that I'm gonna have to sample before the new kids get their greedy maws on my wife.

We all tumble out of the truck, which is parked on the grass near the woods. It's more like a playhouse now, and I smile when I see those purple flowers creeping their way around the tires and winding over the bumpers. I know they're poisonous in high doses, but they look so darned cool that we never bothered to root them out.

And if I really were a trucker poet I'd sigh and rub my square jaw and think about how sometimes prettiness and poison can go together, just like it did for our story. After all, from the poison of our past Quinnie and I built a life that's pretty like a painting. A life where her share of the properties was enough that we could live on this Lake Forest estate, raise our kids right, give them the time and attention and love that will launch them into their own lives with a strong foundation, something neither Quinnie nor I had.

But we have it now, I think as our family giggles its way to the back porch for salad-green sandwiches overflowing with bacon and mayo and a little bit of Quinnie's secret spicy sauce that makes the kids hop up and down and scream for more.

Yeah, we have it now.

A foundation that was built ten years ago, built by the risks we took, the choices we made, the future we saw in each other's eyes outside that nameless gas station.

A future that's here now.

Here forever.

∞

FROM THE AUTHOR

Fun ride, I hope?

Well, press down on the gas, because we're just getting warmed up.

The CURVY FOR KEEPS Series rolls on with PUNISHED BY THE PRINCIPAL!

And if you're caught up, catch up with some of my other super-hot stuff: DRAGON'S CURVY MATE and CURVY FOR HIM!

Or for something slightly less wild (but still a bit out there . . .), try theCURVY IN COLLEGE Series!

Love,
Anna.
mail@annabellewinters.com

∞

Books by Annabelle Winters

The CURVES FOR SHEIKHS Series
Curves for the Sheikh
Flames for the Sheikh
Hostage for the Sheikh
Single for the Sheikh
Stockings for the Sheikh
Untouched for the Sheikh
Surrogate for the Sheikh
Stars for the Sheikh
Shelter for the Sheikh
Shared for the Sheikh
Assassin for the Sheikh
Privilege for the Sheikh
Ransomed for the Sheikh
Uncorked for the Sheikh
Haunted for the Sheikh
Grateful for the Sheikh
Mistletoe for the Sheikh
Fake for the Sheikh

The CURVES FOR SHIFTERS Series
Curves for the Dragon
Born for the Bear
Witch for the Wolf
Tamed for the Lion
Taken for the Tiger

The CURVY FOR HIM Series
The Teacher and the Trainer
The Librarian and the Cop
The Lawyer and the Cowboy
The Princess and the Pirate

The CEO and the Soldier
The Astronaut and the Alien
The Botanist and the Biker
The Psychic and the Senator

THE CURVY FOR THE HOLIDAYS SERIES

Taken on Thanksgiving
Captive for Christmas
Night Before New Year's
Vampire's Curvy Valentine
Flagged on the Fourth
Home for Halloween

THE CURVY FOR KEEPS SERIES

Summoned by the CEO
Given to the Groom

THE DRAGON'S CURVY MATE SERIES

Dragon's Curvy Assistant
Dragon's Curvy Banker
Dragon's Curvy Counselor
Dragon's Curvy Doctor
Dragon's Curvy Engineer
Dragon's Curvy Firefighter
Dragon's Curvy Gambler

THE CURVY IN COLLEGE SERIES

The Jock and the Genius
The Rockstar and the Recluse
The Dropout and the Debutante
The Player and the Princess
The Fratboy and the Feminist

WWW.ANNABELLEWINTERS.

Printed in Great Britain
by Amazon